WELCOME TO MY UNIVERSE

IT IS A LARK

ENTER THE GUARDIANS

LOST

ON

GROT

BY

W. SHANE WILSON

BOOK TWO OF THE GUARDIANS

THIS BOOK IS DEDICATED TO LOVERS OF A GREAT TALE OF HEROES AND THE LIFE THEY LEAD.

TO MY WIFE, MY ONE TRUE LOVE:

FOR ALL THE LOVE AND SUPPORT.

I LOVE YOU MORE THAN MY NEXT BREATH. MAY I ALWAYS DESERVE YOUR LOVE AND MAKE YOU PROUD THAT I AM YOUR MAN.

CHAPTERS:

PRELUDE:

In the wilderness of the planet Grot there is this day a trial of blood leading deeper into the frontier. There is an alien with long matted hair walking in a torn and blood rag that was once a uniform. His steps were erratic and measured because he wobbled and nearly fell with each one he took. His stomach growled and sent a wave of nausea to his already light head. It was not just hunger but a terrible burning thirst.

Tarocs were grazing a mile or so away from the alien who was steadily moving their way. Tarocs are a four horned herd animal. They have two horns that jut out below their lower jaw and two that extend just above their big round red eyes. A Tarocs weighs around two thousand pounds; they are hunted for food by the Grot. Tarocs are therefore skittish about strangers or anything that is not one of them. At present the herd was drinking water and eating the wild fruit near the water to fatten up for the herd movement to the east, where they would mate.

The alien walked right up to a huge Tarocs and looked at it. If the animal could eat the fruit is was not poison he thought to himself, and then again I am not one of them. What if this is not my world and I crashed here? Oh the hell with it, the alien's stomach lurched and the alien convulsed with pain at not having had any food in way to long. The alien decide to chance it, starvation was not way to die. The fruit was juicy and delicious, and the juice ran down the alien's face and on to his chest. The alien reached up and scratched the Tarocs right between its eyes. The normally skittish animal just closed its eyes and enjoyed the scratch and even grunted its pleasure. Side by side the animal and the alien enjoy a meal, the then the Tarocs led the alien down to the water to drink and wash the juices off their faces.

As the day waned the alien followed his new Tarocs friend to the east away from the Grot city some twenty six miles away. At night the alien saw the lights but it bought no interest to him.

(Elsewhere on Grot)

Elon was in chambers with his father the king about the growing unrest in the galaxy and the requests by many planets to aid them if war broke out. One major problem was that both side wanted them as allies. Therefore that was the main subject of their conversation. The king being wise knew Elon to be a better expert on the Non-Grot worlds and the races that lived there. He would have the prince decide who the Grot would back. Elon would no doubt pick the winning side and stay out of harms was. The guardians were closer to the Grot than they had been in years, so they would side with the Grot as well. Being the King of the Grot was a good deal right now.

"Excuse the interruption your kinglyness" Said a big brute of a Grot Page.

"Yes".

"Pardon the bad news, but I was directed to come and tell you immediately if any news ever involved the tome of Brig the hero" The Page said.

"Well, what is the news" Elon asked?

The page began to shake with fear of the retribution of the mad prince when he explained the nature of the news. The prince noticed he was stalling and stamped his massive foot to get the pages attention.

"Sorry, but the tome has been ripped open and the body of the hero is gone" the page said.

"Oh MY GOD; Then we are at war with the Kylr. Spread the news, we are at a state of alert until I countermand that order" Elon yelled. "I will go get Jar and we will look at the tome together".

Jar was shaken at the news; he silently followed Elon to the tome. They saw the tome ripped apart and the crystal coffin was shattered and lay in fragments all over the place. It was blasted apart, no missing that, both of them are experience warriors, so they saw that right away... The thing that threw them was the blood leading not to the port and ships, but out toward the frontier and the waste lands

CHAPTER ONE: WILDS

Farther into the wilderness went the alien. He followed the Tarocs as they moved to the breeding grounds that they went to every year for as long as they lived. The huge herd animals seemed to not only; not mind him; but they seemed to have decided to adopt the tiny alien as one of them. The Tarocs were peaceful they did not fight among themselves, so the alien was worried that if a predator came up on them they would be killed far too easily. He must protect his new friends. As the days rolled by; the alien slept ringed by the huge Tarocs, a living wall around him so he could sleep without being jumped by a predator of scavenger. The alien thought this was backwards since the Tarocs were a peaceful nerfy animal that did not seem to understand fighting or defense of any kind. Moreover, for all their huge size they did not seem to eat over much, it occurred to the alien that he consumed more actual food than the giant four horned cattle animal.

The wilds of Grot were a rich purple and deep red hue, it was breath taking. The alien vaguely remembered blues and greens from another world but could not explain how or where he got the knowledge from. The flyers in the sky were a cross between birds and reptiles, they were a yellow blue combination, and elegant to watch as they dipped and banked at high speeds while hunting for food. There were various rabbit type critters all around the plains and brush, so both the flyers and medium sized hunters would eat well enough. Water was also in good supply, as were fruits and berries of an exotic nature, very tasty and colorful. A low growl came from the brush and the Tarocs moved fast away from the undergrowth, all except the Tarocs that had first bonded with the alien, it stood with its head down horns out, eyes narrowed. The alien had thought them peaceful, then again perhaps not if the need arose, or they were protecting their young. Was that how the Tarocs thought of him, as a child because of his tiny size? The thought made him laugh out loud. The Tarocs looked at him without turning its heavily muscled neck and head. The alien scratched his friend between his upper horns, just how the animal liked it.

The brush erupted in a blur of fur and claws. An animal that was a cross between a bear and a lion roared at the Tarocs and took a swipe at the herd animal. The Tarocs side stepped and then rammed all four horns into the predator's ribs knocking the stuffing out of it temporarily. The beast got up fast, too fast for a huge killer of at the least one thousand pounds;, it turn on the alien and the Tarocs stepped in front of the bear-lion and snarled. The alien was shocked at the sound coming from the timid beast. The bear creature had the bulk muscle of a bear and the speed and agility of a lion, not a good combo for the prey, it was called a Grim'oc, and it had red-black fur and was ten foot tall standing up with four inch claws jutting from every paw foot.

The alien knew that the Tarocs skin could not withstand the claws of the Grim'oc, but the giant bull was not about to back down. It was baffling why the animal wanted to fight an obviously superior opponent. The Grim'oc bear slapped the Tarocs on the shoulder, blood sprayed all over the alien, the Tarocs rammed forward and hit the Grim'oc in the stomach tear it open in two nasty rips and launching it 15 feet into the air and down hard in the field. The Tarocs was about to charge when the alien grabbed its lower horns and held it still looking it directly in the eyes.

"Hold my friend Tarc, you have done enough" the alien said.

The alien walked around flipped his hair out of his face and placed his hands over the gash on the Tarc's shoulder and hummed. Tarc shied away a little, but held his ground once the pain was ebbing away and the wound closed. When the alien took his tiny hands away there were no wound only a new fourteen inch long jagged scar.

The Grim'oc jumped on to its feet ignoring the wounds applied by Tarc, and dove at Tarc and his tiny alien companion. The giant powerful killer was surprised when the alien attacked instead of retreating. Tarc was startled at the show of such fierce combat skills. Tarocs are not dumb animals, they are thinking creatures and it was a spectacle watching the Grim'oc and alien fight in a whirlwind of blood and claws.

The alien picked up a bone that he found on the ground from a month old kill, it was still strong and rigid without being brittle. The tiny alien used it like a bamboo cane or boken; he beat the Grim'oc about the head and eyes and then stabbed it in the rear leg so the mighty beast could not put weight on that leg to launch its weight forward. Tarc watched at first in fear of his little friend, then in awe of him. The tiny man was incredible, he knew just where to hit the Grim'oc to do the most damage and take the least damage to himself. In the end there was so much blood it was impossible to tell who was winning.

The Grim'oc roared and walked away toward the brush, it collapsed just before the edge of the foliage, and the Grim'oc was dead. The tiny alien was lying on the ground breathing like a racehorse after the derby. He was alive and covered in blood, and he almost seemed to be glowing. Tarc went over and nudged the little fellow, who opened his eyes and reach out and stroked the place between Tarc's horns just how he liked.

"He was one mean bastard Tarc, but I could not let him win or he would have killed you" The alien said softly.

The alien pulled himself up by pulling on Tarc horn to helping him. He looked around on the ground for awhile, until he found a flat sharp edged rock. He felt it and turned it over in his hand inspecting it, finally satisfied that this was the right tool for the job, the alien set upon the Grim'oc. He skinned the massive beast in a quick and efficient manner, like he had done this before. Tarc noticed that even when the tiny man was fighting the Grim'oc, he seemed to have no malice in him, and that he killed the bear-lion because he had no choice. When the skin was free of the bear, the alien scrapped it clean for about an hour, then he folded it up and carried it away as he followed Tarc in the direction of the herd. Tarc finally stopped and spoke.

"My small friend, you need to climb on my back, you're too tired to continue; you saved my life after all. Your weight on my back is nothing; fear not." Tarc said in a deep husky voice.

"I did not know you could speak" The alien said?

"We don't usually speak to any but our own kind and I am not sure how you can understand me, but you do" Tarc said.

"Well, thank you Tarc, I am exhausted, that bear was a handful, I was not sure if I could take him. He was stupid and that made the difference in the end" The man said "You're not speaking my language; not even close, but I do understand you. It sickens me to think of your being hunted for food, my God your intelligent beings".

"It is not the Grim'oc that is the problem, it is the Grot, and this is their world. They used to shoot us with big guns, but it was too easy; so now they hunt us with blades and spears, because it makes them work harder. We don't like it but it does serve to keep a balance among our numbers I suppose" Tarc said.

"I take it back, your extremely smart beings, not merely intelligent. This is not my world either, but I don't even know who I am, or what I am." The alien said.

"You're trained in the art of survival; and combat of some sort, yet, you have a gentle nature, however your spirit appears as a raging inferno to us. We Tarocs find you a mystery, but one we want around. You're a meat eater but do not seem to want to kill and eat us, that is odd to us" Tarc said.

"It is rude to eat your friends Tarc, I am content to eat fruits, berries and what ever God can provide for me to eat now, but you're not on my menu and you never will be. You have my word." The alien said as he yawned and closed his eyes. He was fast asleep the whole way to the herd.

CHAPTER TWO: FALLOUT.

In the days that followed the discovery of Brigand Sawyer's tomb being robbed Elon and Jar tread very carefully on the subject. It was a guarded state secret that was so important that the penalty for disclosure was death. Jar was asked to explain the situation to Jamis in private. Jar traveled to Kyl to explain in person, which would remove the chance for anyone to listen in on the conversation. Privacy was a must.

Jar walked down the gang plank and was greeted by Bello who looked angry, well more than his usual scowl anyway. He walked up to Jar and took him by the arm and walked him at the quick step to Jamis's private chambers. Bello did not speak; neither did he depart when Jar and Jamis sat down to converse. Jar looked at him, Bello glared back.

"This is to be a private audience Bello, please leave" Jar said.

"No".

"That was an order Bello" Jar said

"You are not in charge anymore Jar, myself and Rok are the deputy commanders of all the Guard, and Korln is our chief, therefore, you are not giving me or anyone else orders today" Bello said dryly.

"Let us get to the crux of your visit shall we gentlemen" Jamis said.

Jar looked physically ill, he took several moments to calm himself and find the proper way to start the explanation, that might lead to all out war. He noticed that Bello was observing him with a skeptical eye, as was Jamis. If Jar did not know better he was think that they already knew what he was going to tell them. Jar basically decided that he could wait no longer and spoke.

"Brigand Sawyer's tomb has been violated, his body is missing, Elon is searching the planet and the near by systems for any sign of Brig." Jar said sourly.

"Were you not watching and maintaining a guard on his tomb" Jamis inquired?

Jar looked nervous to the point of vomiting; he was avoiding looking into either Bello's or the speakers eyes. He cleared his throat and looked up.

"I advised the king that there was no reason to guard a dead man's body, so King Elor removed the soldier from his post, I did not believe that Brig's remains needed a guard, he is dead and has left all of his enemies behind." Jar said in a rush.

"Oh, I see. So you still harbor ill will against the very man you made a guardian, you better search your heart and soul son and find what is within. You have betrayed the sacred trust of your brethren by allowing Brig's grave to be violated." Jamis said in a quiet tone. "Bello, take Rok and investigate personally please. DO NOT let Korin and Jillian hear of this or death will rain down on all of our heads, such is their passion."

"Rok's and mine passion is no less, we will get to the bottom of this, in spite of lack luster performance from the few" Bello said as he turned to stomp out of the room.

(Elsewhere at the Academy)

The student went flying on to his back, having been thrown again by the slight form of Korin. Rok just smiled knowing that only Jillian ever gave Korin a run for her money, they were the only two with the agility and reflexes to challenge the other. The new Guardians had much to learn, they still relied on strength of body, instead of strength of spirit, and thus Korin beat them easily. All of them, in a row without rest. The students were angry and irritated at being played with like children.

"Why don't you teach us something useful, like how to use our G-jen to kill" A student said.

Korin would have killed him where he stood if not for Rok's timely intervention. Rok backhanded the student in a blur of movement that only Korin could follow. Before the Guard hit the ground Rok's massive foot slammed him into the ground and pinned him there hard. The orange glow Rok was beaming; was frightening, because it enhanced his menace.

"If you can not defend yourself without your G-jen boy, then you can't defend yourself at all. That piece of metal on your arm does not give you the right to take lives, it say you are the LAW, THE LAW! If you disgrace the Guardians, I will kill you personally" Rok Boomed.

"I am sorry" The student said.

"One additional thing children (none of them were kids, only adults can be guardians do to the painful nature of the G-jen placement, a death sentence), Korin is by far the most powerful of all the Guardians and it is she who rules the Guard so respect her or pay the price" Rok growled.

Bello walked in and motioned to Rok that he wished a quick word. Bello escorted Rok out of the building so Korin would not overhear what he was going to say.

"Brig's tome was ripped open and his body is gone. We have to go and settle this matter quietly or there will be all out war that can not happen, not at any cost. We have to find and retrieve Brig's body and lay him back to rest with all possible haste, Korin and Jillian must never know" Bello said.

"When do we leave" Rok said.

"Now, Milo is waiting to take us, we better leave fast before Korin get wind of this" Bello said.

Milo was indeed waiting for them, he must have known by the look on his young face that Bello's need was grave, because he looked years older and meaner just then, Rok thought. Even after his death Brigand Sawyer had a far reaching touch Rok observed.

(On Grot)

Prince Elon was furious; he had just learned that the eternal guard that was to be walking post was relieved of duty and sent elsewhere. This was not what Elon had agreed to, and the Guardians would look upon this as treason, a willful act leading to war. The King was nearly cowering in the face of Elon's wrath. The Grot royal guard was sent out and they nearly ran to get out of there as fast as they could. Elon had a horrible temper once set off he was deadly.

"DO YOU UNDERSTAND WHAT YOU HAVE DONE" Elon screamed!

"I am king of the Grot I do not need your permission to act" Elor countered.

The king was hit in the chest so fast he did not know it had happened until he was tumbling head over tea-kettle. He slammed into a wall and was going to rise but Elon was already there standing over him with a deadly glare and intent. The king wisely stayed on the ground so he would not be killed. The cuff was hard but not lethal, he knew very well that his son could have took his life with a single mighty blow, yet he did not, the king wondered why he still was breathing?

"If our people are to survive this fiasco, we had better find Sawyer's body before the guardians do, or God save us from Korin's wrath." Elon said, and then he reached out and lifted the king off the ground with one hand, with no effort at all.

"I will be more considerate of your counsel in the future" Elor said.

"I have no desire to be king my father, but I can not allow our people to be butchered as a result of a simple mistake, was Jar part of the decision" Elon asked?

"Yes".

The crown prince made a stern face that promised retribution for Jar when he met the guardian again, Elon was not forgiving by nature and Jar seemed to be meddling in Grot home world affairs. Jar was therefore going to have to be eliminated from the equation all together.

CHAPTER 3: SEARCH FOR THE BODY

In Milo's rush to leave for Grot he forgot to say hello and farewell to Jillian who was his dear friend. Oru had not been seen in months, it was thought he would never return because Brig was dead and Jillian was strong enough to defend herself, thus the Wira felt unnecessary and left for God knows where. Oru however, never stopped watching over Jillian. Oru was a dark sentinel, lurking in the darkness and crags in the hills, waiting until he was needed and then there would be hell to pay, for the Wira had a well spring of anger in his heart, he hated everyone but Korin and his own Jilly, and mostly he hated himself for not being able to save his bonded soul mate Brigand Sawyer.

(On the Kyl Ship Gato)

Bello and Rok were trying to make Milo understand that the situation must be dealt with quietly to prevent galactic war, blame meant nothing if they could not stop the war from starting, right or wrong, no matter what Brig's body must be found and laid back to rest in the tome.

"Bullshit, who ever took Brig, I am going to choke the life out of them" Milo said through clenched teeth.

Rok looked at Bello and then spoke.

"Only if you beat us to them son, if not there will be nothing left to choke, you have my word on it. I am no less miffed than you, I want the heads of the guilty, but those heads are in some part

Jar's and the king of the Grot Elor's, so caution is a must for now at least" Rok explain in his baritone voice.

"It matters not who is to blame Milo, if we don't find Brig damn fast, then Korin and Jillian will go to Grot and raze the planet in a day. So at all costs we must BE QUIET about our mission or we will be doing damage control for years to come" Bello said flatly

The orbit of Grot was giving off weird energy readings. The first mate called to Milo to report it. Milo and the two Guardsmen went to the bridge to look into the occurrence.   Sure enough there was a constant energy flux, to much for a satellite or even a weapon, which the Grot did not use; because they like to fight you face to face, long range weapons were cowardly to them. Rok suddenly jerk straight up and jumped to a console off to the side.

"What is it Rok" Bello asked?

"Just a thought, give me a second" Rok answered.

It only took a few minutes and the giant turned to look at his friends.

"Cloaked ship, I am positive of it now. I check an old ships log in the archives and it talked about just what the reading are showing presently. There is a ship out there somewhere cloaked and unannounced in Grot space. Things just went from bad to worse" Rok explained.

"Change of plans then, Milo find that ship, shields up and full man of war protocols, get them, arrested them if you can , shoot them down if they resist." Bello ordered.

"Wont that start another war" Milo asked casually?

"No, they are breaking the law already; there has been no declaration of war against the Grot filed, so no retaliation can be rendered against Kyl for the action if it has to be taken." Rok explain gruffly.

(On Grot)

The Tarocs were nearing the grounds where they went to rut and mate and enjoy some peace. No predator had ever been there, it was known that the Tarocs were dangerous and vicious during mating season. Moreover, the Tarocs great size and four horns plus wrath meant bad odds for an attacker. The alien was the first actually predator ever allowed in, the decision was made while the tiny man slept. The Grim'oc hide that was being carried by the man was frightening at first, but the Tarocs calmed down when Tarc told them of how the tiny person claimed the hide by ritual combat and with nothing more than a bone he defeated the monster. The many Tarocs herds came by to see the tiny alien that killed a mighty Grim'oc hunter; and some scoffed, but most just inclined their massive head in a show of respect and envy. The Tarocs made a powerful friend in this small light weight alien and all was well with the world at that moment for them.

(In the capitol city of Grot-lorzel)

Elon called on the many bounty hunters on his planet, Grot and alien. He gathered them up and explained the need to find the body now and intact if possible. Further, if the body thieves were found they were to be brought back ALIVE, dead paid nothing. Elon drove this point home thoroughly. One of the hunters was a dangerous alien from a race called the Karna, a humanoid race that was feline in nature. They did not look like cats; they stood upright and looked human except for their tail and black stripes that ruled their bodies. This one was a female named Tigra, she was ruthless and deadly, even Elon was careful around her.

"I called on you Tigra because you have never failed to complete a mission, your record is perfect" Elon said.

"If you think the tome breakers are in the wilds of Grot, then I will get them, if they are off world then we will see. I will start on the planet first, to rule it out" Tigra said.

"Very good little lady, but I want them alive if you please" Elon said.

Tigra smiled at him and walked away. She was exotic to the extreme. She stood 6 foot tall, 145lbs, raven black tresses that went down to her hard muscled butt. Her body was lean hard muscle, she was faster than almost anyone and she trained in every lethal art she could learn. So, her body was a work of art. She did have fine scars over her hands, feet and body, but it made her somehow more desirable not less. The problem with Tigra is she lived to hunt, so a private life was out. She did not like to kill only hunt, but she was among the greatest predators in the universe. She went to the tome and inspected it first hand, most of the bounty hunters just scattered randomly hoping to turn up something. Fools. Tigra did not believe in luck, she believed in hard work and deduction.

The Grot soldier looked at her with disdain, most Grot being huge and powerful looked down on other races less physically gifted, Tigra actually was amused by the foolish behavior, and this moron would be dead before he could even react to her if she attacked him. Tigra saw something that threw her for a loop.

Had nobody seriously looked over this tome? No one broke into it; it was broken from the inside. Tigra knew of no Tech that could do this with out destroying what was within, therefore the only conclusion was that Brig was somehow undead and broke out. That conclusion was insane but it was as good as any other. The scent of blood led out in the wilds of Grot. Tigra smiled and gathered her gear.

"So it is to be the hunt, good" Tigra said to herself and set off into the wilds of the gigantic planet.

A two man team of aliens on air gliders; who were both Mercs, were the first to see the Tarocs from the sky, they thought it would be fun to drop down and shoot a few of the large herd beasts. Little did they know that their span was up? They did indeed drop out of the sky and dive-bomb the herd. A rock hit the first one in the left eye, he lost control and hit his partner and they went down hard into the ground, neither would ever rise again. The tiny alien ran over and tossed soil on the burning wreckage. The Tarocs watched in interest.

"If a predator or more of these flying men see the smoke they will come here and you might be killed, we have to put the fire and the smoke out fast" The alien explained.

"Move my friend" Tarc said as he lowered his big horns down and plowed the soil up and over the wreckage, other Tarocs helped.

The alien took the weapons of the bounty hunters and looked them over, the blasters were useless, but they had very nice blades, they matched. The dead were bigger aliens that the tiny one who claimed their knives for himself, so they were more like short swords to the tiny man. The little alien moved and practiced with the blades for a few minutes, the Tarocs moved away. Tarc came over and spoke for them.

"Your skill with a blade is magnificent little friend, and it terrifies them though, you remind them of the Grot butchers that hunt us" Tarc explained.

"I am going to use these bladed to protect you, I will not draw your blood, and I give my word" The alien said "The thought of eating a being that can talk to me is repulsive". The alien stated flatly.

The Tarocs gathered around the alien and each one rubbed him softly with their heads, a sign of trust and endearment. Tarc explain later that a non-Tarocs has never been shown that level of trust, because no outsider was ever trusted. The alien was moved by the gesture visibly.

That night the tiny fellow watched the sky, there was something chewing on his mind, he could almost grasp it, and then it would flutter away into the void in his mind. Why couldn't he remember who he was and why he was here? This was not his world, he knew that beyond a doubt, if that was so, then where the hell was his world; suddenly and once again the void, no answer to his queries. Tarc was walking around the herd to make sure no predators snuck in and made off with one of the smaller members of the great family. Tarc was another unknown quantity; he was not timid or shy, more he was willing to fight instead of run, this was no the Tarocs way. The alien thought for along time. The stars were so beautiful, as he fell into a light slumber he saw two beautiful faces smiling at him, it caused him such a stab of pain that he work up instantly with tears on his face, yet he did not know why. Tarc was lying on ground by him, neither talked; they just let the night take over and dropped off to sleep.

The morning came with a burst of golden sunlight and the Tarocs began to move along to the valley that would lead them to their breeding area. There were signs of Grim'oc hunting in the area, but they stayed away, likely because the hide of one of their cousins was hung over the shoulder of a tiny wasp of an alien with two shiny blades that were visible for miles.

Miles away Tigra could see the occasional glint of steel against the sun, she knew that someone was out there; and she paid little attention because of the great number of bounty hunters crisscrossing Grot. Later, she would realize that was who she was looking for, and the end of her journey, and a good payday. However, that time was not now.

CHAPTER FOUR: SNAKE HUNTER.

In the wilds of Kyl, which were as beautiful as any wilderness on any planet, a lone figure faces off with a deadly Snakoid. The massive forty foot long furry snake with rows of venom dripping razor sharp teeth, waited until the figure made their move. The Snakoid was not stupid; many of his kind were lying out in the sun rent apart by the mighty Glave wielded by the feral child standing before him. The Snake wanted to kill the child and go back underground, but if the Snake tried to just leave the child would gut him. Even if the Snakoid managed to slip by the child she would drop explosives into the ground and blow the large snake apart, therefore, retreat was not a possible option. If he wanted life, then he must deliver death to the child first class.

"Come on you big stupid worm" The child yelled!

"What is a worm" the Snakoid said to himself, because no creature spoke his language?

"My lover died from your poison, so every single one of you are going to die as well to make up for it" Jillian screamed.

The sudden movement of the child was swift, to swift for the big monster snake to counter, she was on him in a single beat of his mighty heart, and he knew for sure his life was over. The snakoid had never killed for fun, he ate everything he was forced to kill just to survive, no wasting, he had shunned civilization for the wilds and he never attacked the Kylr. Today, he was being butchered for sins he did not commit, he wanted to cry out for mercy but he could not make himself understood to the mad child with the deadly hacker.

"Wait, please" The Snakoid thought with all it's mind.

Jillian hesitated because the snakoid closed its eyes and lowered its head right to the ground. It did not want to fight. Jillian stood there looking at the thing, she was for the first time conflicted about her mission to kill all Snakoids. The snakoid opened one eyes and looked at her. It never lifted its huge head, it stayed humble and on the ground, under Jillian's deadly Glave blade. The snakoid opened its maw and out come the tongue super slowly, Jillian watched it come up and hesitate, and then the tongue touched her forearm and suddenly Jillian understood.

"Please don't kill me, I have done no harm." The snakoid stated directly into Jillian's mind.

"You can communicate." Jillian asked?

"Yes, but only by touch with those who are not our race." The snakoid stated.

"My mate was killed from one of your kinds poison and there is no cure for it known. Therefore, I have been killing your kind so no one ever has to loose their lover to that again." Jillian said.

"Balderdash, if you need the antidote to our poison, I will provide it. You see we bit often by accident or in defense so we must be able to undo our bites just in case." The snakoid stated.

Jillian did not look like she believed the snakoid, it understood this clearly. So the huge snake made a suggestion.

"I can demonstrate if you like, but you must take a chance and trust me, there is no other way" The snakoid said.

"Okay, how are you to convince me" Jillian asked.

The answer to her question was simple, the snakoid bite her arm hard, but not the one with the Glave. It hurt so bad Jillian almost puked from the pain and her knees almost buckled. The snakoid lifted its tongue back to her arm the one just bitten.

"Are you in great pain, so you know I have bitten you and you are dying clearly" The snake asked?

"Yes" Jillian managed.

"That is enough to make my demonstration properly" The snake said.

The tongue convulsed and a yellow sweet smelling liquid came out of a gland in the taste buds; instantly Jillian's pain was gone and the wound began to heal over.

"You will be weak for a time so I will carry you back to the city on my back so you can explain to the Kylr that we are not stupid cruel beasts, we are just misunderstood and tragically if it were not for your mate's demise, we would never have been able to explain the truth." The snakoid said.

The Snakoid wrapped its tail around Jillian and gently placed her on its huge soft back and set off for Kyl-prime.

(In the Air above Jillian)

Oru had been looking for Jillian for a few days, the tiny human female moved around a lot and was harder to track than any animal, she was the true hunter now; the mistress of the wilds. Only a fool would hunter this hunter, but Oru was a friend and he wanted to be with her. He had news. Korin was not on the planet anymore and Oru had heard rumors that Brig's body was stolen form his grave. Oru was bonded to Brigand sawyer and would kill anyone who touched his beloved soul mate, no matter the personal cost. Oru was leaving for Grot and Jillian must be told.

Below the Oru-dragon was the strangest sight Oru had ever seen in his long life. It looked like a Kylr riding a Snakoid. Oru swooped down to take a closer look. The Wira monkey panicked when he saw the Snakoid had Jillian in its coils. Oru dropped like a meteor on the snakoid and would have slain it if Jillian did not scream at him at just the right moment.

"ORU STOP" Jillian screamed!

The snakoid was being very careful to make sure Jillian was not injured. Oru was confused. Jillian quickly explained, the Wira did not believe it, so the snakoid touched him with its tongue and Oru was amazed and ashamed of his actions. After a few brief apologies, the three made their way to the city. A few Guardians came out to the edge of the city but they kept their distance, Jillian was universally feared and the Wira was not to be tested unless death was your wish. They came into town with a deadly Snakoid, and Jillian rode it?

(ESLEWHERE IN THE MEDICAL LAB)

Kerra was in the middle of an experiment when a lab assistant said there were a City guard and a guardian outside demanding a moment of her time. Kerra was not in a good mood.

"Tell them to piss off, I am busy" Kerra snapped.

"It is about Miss Jillian" The assistant said.

Kerra's face turned white, which looked odd on a Kylr, since they are blue skinned. Kerra thought Jillian had finally been killed so she dropped the experiment and ran to the doors; and on to the hallway.

"What has happened guardsmen" Kerra inquired?

"Please come with us, Madam Jillian needs you desperately" the Guard said!

Kerra fearing the worst did not argue she just grabbed a medical bag of her own design and supply and followed the guard to the transport.

Jamis was already on the ground with Jillian when the transport arrived. Kerra stepped out and immediately pulled her pistol blaster and shot the Snakoid. Like a snap of chain lightning Jillian caught the blast with her Glave Blade sword and sent it into the sky. Jillian was furious at Kerra until she recognized her.

"OMG Kerra, I have made the most important discovery ever. The Snakoids are not our enemy and they are not stupid beasts." Jillian said in a rush as she smiled at Kerra for the first time since Brig died. "I have the antidote to snakoid poison Kerra"!

"What, that is not possible. I have looked for the antidote for years without success how can a child and an alien child at that best me at research in medicine" Kerra said in a haughty way?

Jillian's happy face was once again grim and Kerra was suddenly scared of Jillian. Wisely Kerra stepped forward and hugged Jillian. She leaned back and kissed her gently on the lips.

"I am sorry Jillian; I am very tired and stressed out these days. The galaxy seems to be holding its breath and waiting for something, I wish I knew what" Kerra explained.

"You are forgiven Kerra, I am happy that I could make a small discovery for the greater good. I am however not the one to be thanked for the information, he is" Jillian pointed at the snakoid.

Jamis was standing next to the Snakoid and he was from the way it looked being bitten. The Guardian was about to destroy the snakoid when Oru grabbed him in his huge Ape form and pinned his arms to his sides.

"No Keel sneek, not enemy, friend" Oru snarled!

"I am well, everyone calm yourselves, this fine creature was explaining how they can help us and how we can help them." Jamis said in his usual calm manner. "Bring me a universal translator".

"That won't work Jamis our father, they don't speak" Kerra said.

The old speaker just smiled at his daughter and took the translator from the guard and made some adjustments to it and then placed it between the Snakoids eyes.

"How is that my friend" Jamis asked/

"I understand you small one, do I make equal sense to you" The Snakoid answered?

"Yes indeed. Now about the cure for your species deadly poison" Jamis asked?

"I demonstrated it for the snake hunter, with the magic cleaver, but all of us have a gland in our tongue with the best curative known. The fluid will heal anything we have ever seen, would you like to see for your selves" The snakoid asked?

There was a shuffle and a Kylr of impossible age came forward carrying a child with the worst full body burns Kerra and

Jillian had ever seen before. The man walked up to the snakoid and put the child down on the ground. He looked up with pleading eyes.

"Help him, he is all I have" The man said?

The huge four thousand pound snake slipped his tongue out and touched the boy who seemed unconscious; the snakoid snapped his tongue back in its massive maw.

"Bring a basin or tub of some sort fast as you can, this boy is dying now" The snake said in a commanding voice!

The gathered crowd looked as if they were baffled. Jillian however was not. Se saw a bubbled out window on a shop down the street. Jillian ran down there and with one swift movement and cut the window out in a perfect glass-steel bowl human sized. Oru who had followed her grabbed it up even though the edges were still hot from the Glave blade. The window was projectile proof and damage proof, but that did not include the famed Glave blade sword, which most could not use even a little; and Jillian was a master of.

"Good, now place the child in the basin quickly Oru" The snake said.

The Wira picked the child up so carefully as if the boy would break if he did not; Oru placed the boy in the warm glass-steel tub and stood back.

"Do not interfere under any circumstances if you want the boy to live" The snakoid stated.

The snakoid put its head over the tub and stuck out its tongue. The crowd moved forward to watch more closely. The giant snakoid's tongue convulsed and a yellow liquid came out a hidden opening in the tongue. The basin began to fill slowly with the fluid. The child opened his eyes and looked up at the snakoid without fear. Jillian came forward; she knelt down and began bathing the child in the healing fluid.

"There does that feel better child" Jillian asked?

"Yes it does, I have not been able to see or even look around for a long time" The child stated.

The look on Kerra's lovely face was priceless. Jamis just smiled wryly as usual. The father of the boy cried un-restrained as the child's skin and burns were healed and closed before the watching eyes of the Kylr.

"The child's eyes are also scarred, place some of the liquid in his eyes and they will be healed as well." The giant snakoid said softly.

Jillian did as she was bid. The child rubbed his eyes a few minutes later and nearly fell over with fright.

"I see your eyes are now restored little Kylr, I mean you no harm child, it was I who healed you burns and repaired you body" The snakoid said.

"Snakoids only kill us, they are not our friends my father told me" The boy said.

"Your father was mistaken, as were we all son." Jamis said.

The crowd looked at Jamis who was smiling as he placed his hand on the snakoid's side and patted it.

"We have a great deal of learning to do, I believe. Our new friend the snakoid is now by my own proclamation a protected species.

They are far too valuable to science and medicine to let anything happen to them. Further, they are all to be fitted with a translator so they are not afraid of us and feel the need to fight when approached." Jamis explained.

"Thank you Jamis" The snakoid said.

"What is your name big fellow?" Jamis asked.

"Sarn" The snakoid answered.

Jamis turned the boy and smiled.

"What is your name son?" Jamis asked.

"It is Alfie sir." the boy said.

"Are you well enough to walk child or do you require help getting back to the medical lab where Kerra would like no doubt to examine you?" Jamis inquired.

The boy tried to get up but he found his legs were weak from disuses. Alfie made another attempt and failed. Sarn reached into the tub with his powerful tail and lifted Alfie on to his massive back.

"I will carry the boy." Sarn said. "I can carry the father as well if he so chooses".

"Nnnno, I wwwwwill walk" The father stated.

Jillian was about to follow when Oru grabbed her and held her tight looking at Jamis. The speaker came over and waited until the crowd left following the giant Sarn to the med lab building. Oru spoke in the best clearest voice Jillian had ever heard the Wira manage.

"Jilly, Breeg grave empty, someone teek my Breeg away. Oru kill when find" The Wira said slowly!

"What?" Jillian growled between her teeth.

Jamis took a deep breath and told Jillian all he knew about this incident, he told her he would arrange a ship for her and Oru and asked her not to kill anyone without just cause, even Jar. Oru plainly was not going to promise. Jamis was genuinely afraid Oru would go crazy and he was powerful enough to destroy all of Grot in anger. Jillian was so fierce now that the shy girl who came with Brigand Sawyer no longer existed; sadly she died when Brig did. Jillian was struggling with her inner fire and Oru was no better off. Jamis looked at them and he felt a little bit off balance.

"Please focus on finding Brig and not starting an interstellar war Jillian, please?" Jamis said.

"I am going to promise nothing; except for the guilty; death." Jillian snapped. "Korin must be told."

CHAPTER 5: MISTAKES

In the hours just passed sunrise the feline hunter in all her glory watched the horizon. Far off in the distance was a herd of beasts they were gentle by the look of them. Once in a while her sharp eyes picked up the shadow of something smaller, that is what she looked for now. Tigra was hired to find the grave robbing trash that desecrated a local hero's grave. Tigra really could care less about the details; she just wanted to get paid.

There was a flash again in the distance, metal. Beasts do not use metal. There was a person or being down there among the beasts. Tigra decided to go check out the herd and see if the person knew anything, she might even have to persuade them to talk. Tigra loved to fight; she was the best of the best and had never known defeat. Among her race she was feared and respected. In the hunter community she was equally feared and respected for her abilities and tenacity.

(WITH THE TAROC HERD)

"We are being watched little one." Tarc said.

"Yes, there is a body up in the hills looking down on us. I don't like to wonder about whether we are in danger or not; so let's bring them to us." The alien said.

The tiny alien pulled one of his deadly blades and turned it so it caught the light from the sun and reflected it in the direction of the watcher. He did this three times about one hour apart as the herd moved. When the alien's huge friend Tarc asked him why he did that, the tiny alien smiled and explained.

"I am pointing out the I am still here and moving with you, this will make the pursuer assume that I don't know I am being watched therefore I am being careless. I am going to slip off in to the dark tonight and ambush them before they can hurt the herd." The alien said with a smile.

The tiny alien made a throat cutting gesture with his thumb, and then looked off in to the distance, with a sad but dreamy look. Tarc did not like the idea of killing without a reason, but the tiny alien was very good at using his head to beat an opponent, perhaps he would capture the follower instead of kill them.

As the sun faded into the purple landscape; the Tarocs grazed and then settled in to the night. Tarc watched the alien slip off into the night like a soft breeze over the plains. Tarc hoped his little friend would be okay, he was quite fond of the small person.

Tigra came within two hundred yards of the herd just inside of the tree line. She could smell the many creatures that had passed through here and the few who were still hidden in the dark watching her. Tigra had a sixth sense about danger and it was not lit at the moment. Later, Tigra would wonder how she was taken so completely and so fast.

The alien watched his follower and they were like nothing he had ever seen before. It was a female as well, he could tell by her breasts. The female sniffed the air and looked right at him; however made no move to come toward or take a defensive posture because of him. The alien did not want to fight her, she brought back an odd memory of a blue woman who cried in his arms, and this time the memory did not slip away but remained strong in his mind. The alien decide to capture not kill this female and question her.

The leaves moved just as Tigra lost consciousness beside her. She was limp in the alien's arms in the next instant. The alien had hit her in a nerve cluster in the back of her left ear and he knew that she would pass out without having to injure her further.

(IN THE CAPITAL CITY)

The news that Rok and Bello were on their way to Grot was grave. Even more distressing was the news that the Wira and Jillian; who now mastered the deadly Glave bladed sword were coming as well boded very poorly for the Grot.

"Shit, this is just what I don't need!" Elon said to himself.

The crown prince called for the palace guard. They came running. Elon told them they are to escort any member of the Kylr directly to him, not his idiot father. Elon made a mistake that later he would regret immensely.

(ON THE NEW KYLR FLAG SHIP SAWYERS REVENGE)

"Are we there yet?" Rok asked for the thousandth time.

"Yes we are there and they are expecting us. Look at the war ships out there." Milo said.

Both mighty Guardians of the Kyl looked out into the sector of space just in front of the flag ship and were pissed. It looked like they wanted to fight. Rok began to glow slightly orange. Bello who was more stoic as a person was trying not to glow but he failed in the form of a slate blue-grey glow. Milo was worried, but he was not put off by the show of force as well. Under the current circumstances it was unwise to provoke the already volatile Guardians.

"Calm boys, focus on the reason we came not the arrogant posturing of the Grot Air force." Milo said.

"FINE!" Rok growled.

"We can deal with the Grot later if they need to be punished for their roll in what happened to Brig's tomb." Bello said in a flat dry tone.

   The three friends went to the landing bay and took the captain's shuttle down to the planet to meet with Elon the crown prince who ruled the Grot people despite his father being king.

   Jar did not want to be anywhere near the Guardians when they came to Grot, so he kept the king's company as much as possible. Oh how the mighty have fallen.

   The shuttle landed next to the ship that Elon used to visit Kyl, so they knew the prince would be near by when the were on the ground. Elon might be a mighty warrior, but he was not fool enough to think he could stand up to an angry Guardian, and he was about to face two plus a wily captain of uncommon valor. Delicate was the word for this first meeting, but would the Guardians feel that way as well?

"Good afternoon Kylr, welcome the Grot." Elon said.

   Elon smiled as the Kylr walked up.

(SLAM!)

Rok hit Elon so hard in the jaw that the huge mega pound prince back flipped. Elon landed hard on his chest. Bello grabbed Milo's arm as he made to move to stop Rok.

"You will die if you interfere Milo." Bello said.

Rok let Elon stand up, the Grot was three feet taller and at least a hundred pounds of muscle heavier than Rok, but that did not mean that they were evenly matched. Elon was furious and he was the greatest warrior on his planet, but he was going to loose this test if he took it.

"I guess I had that coming for letting Brig's tomb get robbed. I will take the blame, but I will share it with Jar!" Elon said sternly.

"Enough Rok, Elon is not our enemy...yet." Bello said coldly.

Elon was more leery of Bello with his cold way than Rok with his hot temper. Elon could only imagine the chaos that would erupt when Oru and Jillian arrived. It was beginning to look like war would come to his planet. Korin at least was not involved yet, that was something. Jillian and Korin warned Elon if anything happened to Brigand Sawyer's body they would burn his planet to ash in their wrath. There was no way around it, the Grot dropped the ball in the soup and now they were going to have to eat what they have made, namely a huge deadly mess.

(IN SPACE ON JAMIS's PRIVATE SHIP.)

Jillian was silent for the most part for the entire journey; after she made the one and only call that she needed to make. Jillian called Korin who was at the edge of the universe and told her what had happened to Brig's body. Korin went insane with fury; even from millions of light years away Jillian could feel her green fire burning. Jillian felt sorry the crew of the Kyl ship that was carrying Korin.

"Oru are you okay?" Jillian asked.

"Yees, I no like walls, I want open skees." Oru said glumly.

"We will be on Grot in a few hours and then we can...handle this matter." Jillian said in a hoarse voice.

The Wira knew Jillian meant to kill someone for what had happened to Brig, and he would make sure no matter what; Jillian was not to be the one killed. Oru had never truly let go of his control over his power, but he had decided he would loose no more friends to the veil...even if it killed him.

Jillian was incorrect; the trip only took another forty-five minute. The captain of the small Corvette style personal space craft; came to Jillian with a worried look on her face. Jillian already knew what it was she was going to say, but she listened to the Kylr woman anyway.

"We are surrounded by Grot war ships." The captain said.

"Does this tub have guns and shields?" Jillian asked.

"Yes, of course. Why do you asked?" The captain asked.

Jillian smiled and pointed at the planet.

"Tell them we are here to see Elon, and they had better back off. If they do not, then back them off." Jillian said sternly.

The captain's lovely blue face was almost white at Jillian's suggestion. She did not want to have to be the one who started a war, but neither could she disobey Jillian who was Jamis's adopted daughter. The young female captain would be saved from that choice by a clever Wira.

"Say Jamis sent thees ship to Grot; they let you go to planet then, no fight." Oru said thoughtfully.

"Oru you clever monkey, why didn't I think of that?" Jillian asked brightly.

"Jilly sad and mad, no theenky peace." Oru said.

"Right." Jillian said.

The captain did as she was told and the Grot ships dropped away in a hurry at the mention of Jamis. The super fast Corvette ship landed next to Milo's shuttle and Jillian's face was a mask of anger.

"Boys momma is coming!" Jillian growled as she gripped her Glave.

The ship opened and Jillian and Oru jumped out and landed on the ground. They were too wound up to wait for the gang-plank to extend. They were not more than forty paces when they were jumped by the Grot palace guard. The guard did not just come forth and asked Jillian to surrender and come along...No, they had never seen a person who looked like Jillian and a beast like Oru so they charged them weapons drawn. It was a very bad idea; Jillian's slight size let them believe she would be an easily beaten opponent. They were wrong, so terribly wrong!

"Wait...don't attack!" Screamed the captain from the Corvette hatch.

The first Grot warrior slammed down a huge sword on Jillian's head. He never made it all the way through the swing.

(ROAR!!!!!)

The offending Grot was grabbed by the chest and slammed through the stone landing pad for starships; he was quite dead. Oru had changed; he was now a giant fuzzy dragon.

"Shoot it in the eyes." A Grot officer yelled!

Jillian moved like chained lightning, she ran up Oru's tail and jumped of his front shoulder; her Glave bladed sword made fan blade destroying the projectiles before they could reach Oru. Jillian engaged the Grot blade to blade. The Grot weapons were nothing fancy but they were very durable, the Glave cut deep into them with Jillian's every strike, she fought four on one and the Grot's massive weight and strength would have killed another person. However, Jillian was not a regular person. She had spent a great deal of time fighting huge Snakoids; that were many times the Grot's combined weight and were strong enough to crush the life out of a Grot with no effort. Jillian carried the mighty Glave and was a master of its use. The Grot were on their heels bleeding profusely. Jillian showed no emotion just the way Jamis trained her. Eye on the goal, mind on the combat.

Oru knocked the stuffing out of any Grot that got to close to Jillian's back. He spit fire into the face of a Grot who was lining Jillian up with his lance.

"ORU BACK UP NOW!" Jillian screamed.

The Wira could hear the urgency in Jillian's voice did as he was bid. Jillian swept way down to ground level and the Glave flashed once and then again, the blade grew five times as long as it had been and Jillian attacked with reckless abandon. All the

Grot were killed in less than four seconds. Jillian nearly
toppled from the effort.

"Jilly!" Oru yelled as he lunged forward and grabbed her up into
his powerful dragon arms.

Jillian looked at Oru and slipped into a lite sleep. You see the
power of the Glave blade sword comes from the user, Jillian used
up almost all of her energy in one amazing strike to end the
conflict, it nearly killed her.

"Oru, JILLIAN!" came a booming voice.

Rok slammed into the ground like a warhead; he left a crater
four feet deep. He jumped out of it alert and he ran to Oru in
dragon form and looked at Jillian, then he turned a complete
circle observing the area carefully.

"Dear God what happened here?" Rok asked.

"Jilly." Oru growled in answer.

Rok looked up as Bello dropped right by his side G-jen glowing
Bright. Bello looked at Jillian and his face grew so hard it looked
like stone. It was no mystery the Guardians looked on this event
as a declaration of war. It was not to be though; Jillian opened
her eyes and spoke.

"Food and drink would be greatly appreciated." Jillian said softly.

Elon's sled transport came screaming into the scene with Milo
hanging on to it for dear life. Elon set the sled down and jumped
off it. Milo followed. The prince came up and looked at Jillian
with shock on his rugged face. There were twelve dead Grot
warriors, ten were neatly dissected.

"The Glave?" Elon said.

"Yes. Oru and I asked them not to attack us, we tried to explain that we were here to investigate Brig's tome raiding but they attacked us like wild beasts, so I slaughtered them." Jillian said firmly.

Jillian was suddenly on her feet and the Glave blade snapped out to four feet in length and glowed like the sun.

"It is said that the Glave drinks the soul of the user. This is why nearly no one can use one. I am curious about the amount of power one of those gives you and what it takes from you in return?" Elon asked.

"I can defend myself even against a Guardian, beside them; I have no equal in combat with the Glave in my hand. A word of caution, I cannot be parted with the Glave, we are one." Jillian said.

Jillian tossed the Glave to Elon and the blade instantly disappeared. Elon held it up and there was a slight glow. Jillian smiled, Elon had some inner talent, and the kind of inner strength that would someday make the Glave blaze. Today was not that day. Jillian decided to show off a little to discourage any further attacks on her person. Jillian held out her hand and spoke.

"Ignite." Jillian said.

The Glave burst into flames like a small sun and then it jerked out of Elon's might grasp, it did not fly to Jillian. The Glave made a circle around the assembled group and then went into a complicated series of movement so fast that only the Guardians could see them, and it caused awe to climb into their eyes. Jillian reached out and the Glave snapped into her hand, where it flared and then went silent.

"I do not have to touch or hold the Glave to use it; I am far passed that point. I have totally merged with the weapon; it comes to my call and serves me loyally." Jillian explained.

Bello who was an emotionless person before Brig's valor set a fire in his heart, now Bello had a deep silent passion about being a Guardian and making a difference. His loyalty was to the Guardians and Jillian and no other. Jamis would be proud.

"That was an amazing display of power and skill Jillian; however you still look ill and spent." Bello said.

"Come Jillian mistress of the Glave and I will take you to the palace where you can rest and dine." Elon said.

Three Grot Palace guards ran up and attacked Oru. The Wira looked more confused than angry. The Grot weapons merely bounced off his Dragon scales. Elon was furious, he came around Oru's front leg and grabbed the guard by the head and threw him into the side of the Kyl shuttle across the tarmac fifty plus yards away. Elon turned on the other two guards and screamed at them.

"WHO THE HELL TOLD YOU TO ATTACK OUR GUESTS?" Elon bellowed.

"You gave the order sir, you told us to watch for the Kylr Guardians and escort them. You gave the order that any other intruders be attacked and captured so they can be questioned about the hero's tome." The guard said boldly.

Elon looked ill when he realized that he was to blame, he had made a mistake that cost an entire unit to be killed, and more important the Kylr were on the brink of war with the Grot over Brig's tome being robbed. Life was very complicated right now for Elon, damn Jar and his father for putting him in this mess.

"I will arrange for the families of the guards to be compensated and the dead will be buried heroes of the people." Elon said picking up the guard he hurled into the ship.

The gathered group and went to the palace to eat and rest. Oru sat next to Jillian on the floor as she slept. Elon himself brought her food and a barrel of fresh fruits for Oru to eat. The Wira is able to smell poison and chemicals, Oru did not detect any of either so Jillian ate her fill and then lay down and rested. Strangely, though no one but Oru knew it; the snakoid poison really winded her even though she received the antidote. Jillian was forcing herself to function; she was no longer important; Only Brig's grave robbers meant anything to Jillian now; and they were dead.

Bello and Rok went to Brig's tome after they made sure Jillian was secure and resting. Jar was still no where to be found.

CHAPTER 6: THE HUNTER

Tigra Woke up staked out on the ground spread eagle. She was in the shade on her back. Tigra was very strong so she tried to break the bonds with brute strength, it was useless. There just beyond her grasp was an alien going through the supplies she hid miles away. How did it know where to find her gear? The alien as if on cue turned to look right at her. The alien was the strangest creature she had ever seen. It had brown eyes and long ragged brown hair on the top of its head and on its face but that was all. There was a wild look in the alien's eyes. It came toward her.

"Stay away from me or I will kill you!" Tigra snarled.

The alien actually smiled at her.

"I should think not hunter. You are at my complete mercy presently." The alien said.

It was true; Tigra was in a very bad way. If the alien wanted to torture her or kill her; there was little or nothing she could do. The alien knelt beside her and ran a rough hand over her stomach and then her breasts. Tigra blushed; she had not considered the alien might...

"You have soft downy fur all over your body. Your body is hard with muscle, but your skin is soft as satin. You're very attractive for a killer. Are you after the Tarocs, or are you after me?" The alien asked.

The alien's hand never stopped massaging her body, not in a mean or even suggestive way, it was more like how a lover would touch you to let you know they desire and appreciate your company. Tigra actually liked the way the alien was touching her. Tigra had no time for a lover or even friends in her line of work. She was untouched as a female; she thought she wanted that for herself. She realized she was wrong when her heart lurched as the alien leaned down and kissed her lips suddenly.

"I am sorry, I think you remind me of someone I should be able to remember, but cannot, and you are very pretty. Here drink some water." The alien said.

He held up a water skin to her lips and she drank slowly until she had enough. The alien went down to the water hole and filled a basin full of water and carried it up to where Tigra was. Carefully the alien washed her entire body; he talked to her as he did. Once again he was gentle and his touch was not unpleasant to the Karna female.

"You never answered my question about why you were following the Tarocs herd." The alien said.

"I am not hunting the beasts, but you perhaps are who I am looking for?" Tigra answered.

"Why would you be looking for me?" The alien asked.

The alien washed her faces and her hair carefully, and then he combed her hair slowly. Tigra was becoming unhinged by the conflict in her heart and mind. She was this alien's prisoner, but he treated her like a loved one or mate. Tigra was beginning to feel a desire to be held in this alien's arms, she tried to put the feeling aside but his actions were making it impossible. She realized she wished that he would take her against her will so that she did not have to toil over the choice herself.

"A famous hero was buried on this world and his body was stolen from his final resting place." Tigra explained.

The alien stopped and looked into her cats eyes and grimaced.

"You believe me to be a grave robber? I am not, nor would I ever do something so low down and disrespectful as desecrate a person's grave." The alien said looking directly into Tigra's eyes.

Tigra's heart wrench in her chest, she would believe anything this alien told her. His eyes were so sad and sincere, he did not look as if he knew how to lie; it somehow seemed to be beneath him. In the short time Tigra had been at the alien's mercy, she could feel his goodness. Damn her heart now what is she supposed to do?

"I can't let you go yet girl. It has nothing to do with your mission; you make me remember things that I have forgotten. I can't just let you go before I can grasp who I am, because I don't know." The alien said.

"I am Tigra, of the Karna people. I am a tracker and hunter, never have I been the prey before, you are no simple man to capture me. Many have tried, all of them died in the attempt, yet here I am staked out on the ground completely naked and helpless. I would stay with you as long as you wished, but I have a mission and I must go finish it." Tigra explained.

"No."

The alien got up and walked down to the water, he stripped and washed himself. He took out one of Tigra's small blades and cut the hair off his face. He took a piece of cloth and tied his hair back away from his face. When he came back only his left arm was still covered, it was wrapped in leather from his wrist to his elbow. The alien was as naked as she was. Tigra suddenly guessed why the alien washed himself, he was going to take her, and now she did not want to be forced, she wanted to offer herself to the male of her choice.

"Night is falling Tigra and it is cold, I washed myself so that your sharp sense of smell would not be bothered by my alien scent." The alien said.

"I thought you were going to rape me." Tigra told him.

The alien smiled at her and pulled out a thick hide all rolled up. The alien set the hide on the blanket that Tigra was laying on and built a fire. The flames were more to keep the Grim'oc away than to provide heat. The alien rolled out the hide and he laid down touching Tigra. The hide was warm and the alien put his arm across Tigra and rubbed her tummy with his right hand. Tigra did not know when she fell asleep in his arms, but she knew the moment she woke up.

"I had a dream about you Tigra and in the dream we were lovers. I woke up and there you were." The alien said.

The alien was lying on top of Tigra. His face was nearly touching her and his warm body was pressed to hers and she could tell he was aroused by the feel of his heart beat and other things. He was going to take her.

"No you can't have me I refuse!" Tigra snarled.

The alien placed a razor sharp knife between her breasts. Tigra thought he was going to kill her for refusing to love him. The alien pushed the hide back and sat up. He was very aroused Tigra noticed, and damn her betraying body so was she. The alien surprised her by cutting the bonds on her ankles. He leaned back forward and placed the knife in her left hand.

"I don't..." Tigra started to say.

The alien did not ask her for permission but he did not rape her either. Before Tigra could speak his hands were one her face and his mouth was on hers as well. Tigra was so lost in the moment that when they began to make love, she was only fuzzily aware. Tigra wrapped her legs around his back and loved him back. She managed to cut her hand free somehow with the knife he gave her and then she rolled them both over and she got on top of him. Tigra cut the other wrist free and placed the knife on the blanket above the alien's head, she smile and then they made love the rest of the night. Tigra woke to the sound of his gentle breathing. She was wrapped in his strong arms, her back to his belly.

"You are a strange male, alien. I have never wanted for a physical relationship, yet I surrendered to you willingly?" Tigra said softly to herself in reflection.

"I still don't know who I am, but I am not a villain or grave robber. You are free to continue your journey. I will miss you Tigra, you are very special, but your heart is hard and you needed to open it to grow as a person. You are very passionate when you want to be." The alien chuckled as he squeezed her.

Tigra giggled and that startled her. She tensed and then laughed again. Tigra rolled over and looked at the man in the morning light. Oh my God he was the most interesting male she had ever seen. Tigra did not want to leave him, not now not ever. Tigra kissed him on the lips and a tear escaped her eye. He caught it and looked at her.

"Did I injure you, or offend you in some way?" The alien asked.

"No, I just don't want this moment to pass; I want to feel like this forever." Tigra said.

The alien pressed her head to his hard thin chest and ran his hand lovingly up and down her back, until her silent sobs stopped.

"You can stay or go and I will not be farther, than your heart. Come back to me after you are finished with your duty and we can be together then." The alien said.

"You would want me to come back?" Tigra asked.

"Yes, I am alone out here and I don't know who I am or where I come from." The alien said.

(WITH THE TAROCS HERD)

Tarc was grazing in a huge fertile field when he heard the hum of a sky cycle coming. That usually meant that the Grot were coming to harvest some of the herd for food. That was not the case this time. Three bounty hunters flew over the herd and slowed to look at them carefully.

"Move toward the tree line." Tarc said to the Tarocs near him.

The message was passed on again and again until all the herd was moving toward the trees and cover. The bounty hunters must have been bored and peeved about not finding any sign of the grave robbers, because they decided to shot at random Tarocs without just cause.

The Tarocs began to run. The hunters were shocked by the speed the Tarocs were capable of. In a few moments most of the herd was in the protection of the trees. The few that were not protected by the trees moved fast and at odd patterns. The bounty hunters were actually enjoying the challenge of trying to pick off the huge yet swift beasts when a group of Grot came over the hills.

"CEASE OR DIE!" yelled a Grot officer.

"What do you care if we shoot a few animals for fun?" The hunter said.

The six Grot warriors were heavily armored and armed with pulse rifles that they used to shoot poachers. Those rifles were aimed at the three bounty hunters.

"First of all, they are not stupid beasts, they are likely far smarter than you are. Second, they are a source of meat for the Grot people, the main source. We do not kill them for fun; we hunt them only with blades to thin out the weak ones, so that the herd can grow in strength. Shooting them with blasters is a disgrace and cowardly!" the Grot officer growled.

"So what, that is your problem." The hunter said abruptly.

The Grot leader smiled and pointed at the hunters.

"Shoot them down." The leader ordered.

Five pulse rifles burped at the same time and the sky cycle fell from the air. It was a good thing the hunters were not so far off the ground or it would have killed them. They were sore but alive.

"I will now give you a choice. You can run for the trees while we shoot at you, if you make it to the trees you live if not... Or you can fight a Tarocs with only a blade, once again if you win you live if not? Make your choice scum!" The officer said as the other five leveled the pulse rifles menacingly.

The hunters were tough but not stupid and they already witnessed how well the Grot could shoot. Therefore, that was not an option. So to the man they chose to fight a Tarocs.

Tarc had listened to all of the conversation and came out to meet with the Grot officer on the field.

"If you know we are not stupid animals, then how can you eat us?" Tarc asked.

"We are a violent meat eating race and you taste great to us. However, we would eat any race that is not Grot, so it is not personal. We respect your kind; that is why we hunt you on foot and with only blades, to give you a chance for life." The Grot said.

"I wish I could say that is decent of you, but you are after all killing us. I however accept the contest against these murderers. Which is first?" Tarc asked.

The three mercenary hunters looked at the big four horned cattle like creature and were floored that it spoke the universal tongue. They were not afraid to fight it though. That was their second mistake, or third if you count getting caught by the Grot shooting at the herd.

"I will go first." An odd looking cyclopean hunter said.

Tarc snorted with mirth.

"Begin at your leisure friend." Tarc said.

The hunter lunged at Tarc and the Tarocs leader stayed put, at the very last moment Tarc spit in the hunter's single eye while side stepping his charge. The hunter screamed in anger. Tarc lowered his head and head-butted the hunter killing him instantly.

"Next." Tarc said.

The second hunter pulled out a crossbow and the Grot officer slipped a knife under his throat and lifted a tad.

"Blades only, no projectiles at all." The officer said with meaning.

The hunter tossed the bow aside and pulled out a long dagger, which he showed to the Grot. The Grot approved of the fine weapon.

Tarc stood there as if he was in not danger, no danger at all. The hunter ran at him. Tarc backed up. The hunter drove at Tarc trying to cut his front leg at the knee, Tarc just moved. The hunter ran in and out poking at Tarc, Tarc let the blade rake him, and as it did Tarc spun and kicked his left rear leg out, the hunter was launched a good fifty yards. The hunter was dead before he hit the ground.

"Next." Tarc said.

The last hunter decided to run for it, the Grot commander shot his ass off literally, there was nothing left to sit on after two well placed shots. The Grot picked up the dead and tossed them on their transports.

"They will make a fine stew; and my apologies for their cowardly attack. I would like one day to fight you Tarocs; you have a fine spirit in you." The officer said as he began to walk away.

The officer stopped and turned back to Tarc.

"Have you seen any aliens out here? There was a tomb robbed

near the city and the body of an alien hero was stolen." The officer said.

"Did the hero have a name?" Tarc asked.

"It was Brigand Sawyer, he was a Guardian of Kyl, but he was not a blue Kylr, he was a tiny pinky-tan creature of amazing combat prowess." The officer said with respect.

"I thought Guardians could not be killed?" Tarc said.

"I was told that snakoid poison and the force of a star drive killed him. His last gift was of life, for his comrades and crew. Brigand used the power of his gauntlet to super charge the star drive; he used his own body as the conduit. He was a living battery. He gave his life for this world specifically, so he is our hero as well. Such valor is not common." The officer said.

It seemed to Tarc that the Grot were beyond mercy for the guilty parties in this matter. God help them when they were found by the Grot.

"Good day, good Tarocs." The Grot said.

The Grot flew away off in the direction of the nearest city. Tarc walked back to where the dead Tarocs lay. He lowered his massive head and plowed soil over them. A few other Tarocs came and assisted him in the burials; and then herd moved on.

CHAPTER 7: TIDES OF FATE

In the palace Jillian was woke up by the sound of screaming voices. In less than a single blink of the eye, Jillian was on her feet with her Glave in her hand, blade extended. The floor vibrated and then the ground shook violently. Jillian almost stabbed Oru when he spoke because she was startled. Oru snatched the Glave from her hand deftly, like no other could have ever dared to try.

"Jilly no attack Oru!" Oru said.

The Wira handed the Glave back to Jillian and flipped right side up and landed on the floor beside Jillian. Oru had been a bat hanging on the ceiling watching over her.

"I am sorry Oru; you are not like any other person I know. You are far more dangerous and capable. What is happening?" Jillian asked.

"KORIN." Oru said.

Jillian turned to run; Oru shifted into a giant tiger creature and ran beside her. Jillian grabbed a handful of fur and slung up on his back. Oru waited for Jillian to do just that, because once Jillian was in place; Oru accelerated to four times the speed he was going.

Korin's ship landed, and the Emerald Death or Reaper as she was called; burst out of the hatch once it was open and challenged the entire planet to wage war. She was beyond anger, there is no term for where she was emotionally or mentally. The green corona burst out from here body and everything it touched got trashed by the power. Korin was crying uncontrollably and every time she screamed the planet shook.

Oru ripped around a building and jumped back as a Grot shuttle was hurled into the wall by Korin. Jillian got off and looked at Korin.

"OH MY GOD, Oru she has lost her mind." Jillian said in a rush.

The Grot were being kept alive by Bello and Rok. However neither of them could do anything to stop the juggernaut that was Korin. Korin was so strong as a Guardian that it was believed she could defeat all the other Guardians by herself combined at once, and now she was out of her mind with grief and madness.

"Oh Shit! Jillian NO!" Rok screamed.

The hurricane of power that Korin was bleeding into the world was destroying everything. Jillian snapped the Glave bladed sword out and it pulsed with a strange power; that cut right through Korin's power and protected Jillian from being killed. Jillian forced her way forward with great effort until she reached Korin. Jillian just stood there looking at Korin, who had her weeping eyes closed.

(SLLLLAP!!!)

Korin opened her eyes and was looking into the equally hard eyes of Jillian. Korin stopped the green death and stepped forward and cried in Jillian's arms.

"I have missed you my Korin." Jillian said softly as she ruffled the green eyed titan's hair.

"I have been lost without your love Jillian." Korin cried.

"I want to destroy this place as well Korin, but we need to keep it together until we find Brig's body. If we blast the Grot and the planet; we may never find the truth. Please be patient, when we figure this all out I will stand aside and let you deal with the guilty as you see fit." Jillian told Korin.

"Okay, I will follow your lead baby, until we find the guilty, then they die." Korin said coldly.

Bello and Rok came to the side of Korin and they approached carefully. She looked at them, Korin stepped forward and wrapped her arms as far as they would go around her giant adopted brother's waist, which was not far. Korin shook Bello's hand; and then she knocked him on his ass.

"You knew back on Kyl that Brig was missing and did not tell me." Korin said accusingly.

"Yes it is true. I am mad as hell as well dear Korin, but I want to know what has become of our fallen brother before you destroy the Grot and the planet, so I did not tell you or Jillian. I wanted to be able to tell you something solid when you did come to the Grot home world." Bello said unrepentant.

Korin saw the logic of his thoughts and helped him up. Rok was ready to be punished as well but Korin only punched him in the gut.

"Big dummy." Korin said.

"Why don't we go to Brig's tomb and look at it for ourselves, we are not brutes like the Grot and we can sense things they cannot as Guardians. Oru is also a plus; he will be able to tell us much; that we might miss." Jillian suggested.

The group thought that it was a wise idea to look at the actual tomb for clues. The trip there did not take long. Oru became a dragon and Korin rode with Jillian on his mighty back. Milo, Rok rode on the royal sled with Bello and Elon. The prince stayed away from Korin out of both respect and wisdom. Elon set the sled down just short of the tomb. The prince followed the Kylr from behind, damning Jar with every step for risking his people.

The Wira folded himself down to spider monkey size and jumped on to Jillian's shoulder. When Jillian neared the tomb Oru bailed off and would not go further. Jillian stopped and bent down to the tiny creature.

"What is the matter Oru?" Jillian asked.

"No looky at Breeg's grave." Oru said firmly.

"Okay, I will go look and tell you what I see." Jillian said.

The giant Rok went to the tomb and stopped dead. Bello had the same reaction. Korin walked up and made an unusual face, then she entered Brig's tome. Korin emerged as Jillian entered, Korin stopped her and turned her around and pointed to the walls and doors.

"What?" Jillian asked.

Bello was about to answer her when Jillian screamed.

"ORU!".

The Wira shifted to become a four armed ape giant with tusks. He came ripping into the tome snarling ready to kill. Jillian pointed at the walls and the large gem slab where Brig had been laid to rest.

"Who did this Oru?" Jillian demanded.

"This was done by a G-jen Jillian." Bello said.

   Jillian and Korin looked at Bello with murder in their lovely faces; He was startled to see that amount of poison directed at him.

"Yes, I know Bello, I did not ask what; I asked who?" Jillian said.

"BREEG!" Oru said excitedly.

   There was dead silence and Korin could see the heart of everyone beating at irregular rhythms; hers included.

"What did you say Oru?" Rok said in his baritone voice.

"Breeg, only Breeg do this." Oru pointed at the walls and doors.

   They were all shocked. Bello recovered and felt the need to explain.

"These walls are made from Trillium and Corbonite, they are so strong only your Glave or a G-jen can pierce them. They were used so no would ever disturb Brigand Sawyer as he slept." Bello said.

   Jillian was not listening to him, only Elon was. Elon grabbed his Com and yelled seal off the planet, call out the entire guard and military.

"If Sawyer is walking around he is an abomination and must be captured and killed!" Elon said.

   Rok would have killed Elon where he stood but Korin stopped

him and she addressed not Rok or Elon but Oru.

"Where is your Bondling Wira?" Korin demanded.

"Oru say Breeg that way, I smell heem." Oru said pointing to the wilds.

Korin turned and addressed the group while pulling Jillian to her.

"Is it possible that Brigand has returned soulless from the void? If he has then my lover is dead and gone and he must be stopped. If it is still Brig then we made a horrible mistake and need to find him now and make it up to him. Jillian and I will ride Oru into the wilds. Bello you will consult with Jamis on his thoughts. Rok you are to stay with Elon to keep him from making any rash moves, if he tries kill him! That was an order; all of you make it happen. Milo and the other Captains scan the planet from the air." Korin said in an absolute tone.

Korin looked at Jillian and then kissed her on the lips.

"Once more into the void my love, this time we find our lost man, or we don't come back at all." Korin said softly.

"We are united in mind, body and soul then." Jillian said as she kissed her mate back.

Oru snarled and began to twist in a horrible pain. When Korin reached for him, Oru backed her off with a snap of new deadly teeth. Oru writhed in misery for at least a full minute and half. That was unusual for Oru who could explode instantly into shaped and beings at will. Finally Oru finished his painful transformation, and Korin could not tell what he was supposed to be?

"Oru did something forbidden, he made two creatures into one, and Oru will die soon, but not before Oru find Breeg." Oru told them.

The Wira was twenty five feet high at the shoulders and he had the upper body of a giant four armed ape, and the head of a Wolf-tiger. His lower body was that of a Wolf-tiger as well.

"Oru can run faster than any creature and fight and beat any creature like this. Grot is a mean world, many monsters. Oru kill them all if harm my Jilly, Korin or Breeg." Oru said firmly.

Jillian ran her fingers through the giant Oru monsters hair on his neck and cried. Oru tossed her on his back, and then did the same for Korin. Korin held Jillian tight as Oru bound out into the wilderness.

"Why do the people I love keep sacrificing themselves, for someone else I love?" Jillian sobbed.

The three companions blazed off into the wilderness in search of the impossible, and yet the desperately hoped for.

CHAPTER 8: THE MISTAKE

Bello was in contact with Jamis in moments after Korin ordered him to consult with the speaker and leader of all the Kylr people.

"Jamis it is our combined opinion that Brigand Sawyer broke himself out of the Tomb from the inside and is once again walking among the living, or something of that nature. We fear that the Brig that is, is not the Brig that was and he is dangerous to the universe and must be found. Is it possible that he returned soulless?" Bello asked.

"Are you sure Bello, there can be no doubt that the Body of Brigand Sawyer stirs again?" Jamis asked gravely.

"None sir, none at all; Oru the Wira confirmed that it is Brig and no other that opened the tomb." Bello explained.

"If the Wira who is bonded to the man says that it is Brigand; then it is Brig and we must find him immediately. If he has lost his mind, he could be the most dangerous weapon in the universe, and if he has lost his soul, then he must be killed. Find Jar and advise him please." Jamis said as he cut the link.

For the first time in his long life since he brought the Kylr into power did the speaker feel old and helpless; this was all his fault. He had Brigand buried with his G-jen on his left arm: no Guardian can ever truly die until the damned gauntlet is removed. How could I be so stupid, Jamis thought? The speaker went to the private chambers; that he alone could enter, because it was booby-trapped for anyone else and would not allow entrance. Jamis removed an old wood box from his desk and looked in the box and touched the object inside of it lovingly yet sadly, and then signed deeply.

(ON KYL IN THE MED LAB)

Kerra just finished the serum trials on the snakoid poison antidote Sarn had provided. There were twenty Snakoids in a field just outside the city. Alfie and Sarn went and helped explain the new arrangements between the Kylr and the Snakoids. Sarn was delighted by the response the Kylr gave his species after learning that they can heal a great many things with their yellow fluid. Not only that; but Kerra had discovered that a drop of Snakoid poison in a numbing solution could keep the pt senseless longer with no side effects. Sarn was a hero to his clan and the Kylr both. Alfie was an instant hit with the giant Snakoids; so much so; many of the younger Snakoids asked for riders of their own. Jamis granted them an organizational charter and mandate to roam the wilds of Kyl as rescue and medical teams, because the Snakoids can dig through solid rock and heal nearly any injury save death or severe crushing and so on.

"Kerra, this is your father please come and dine with me this evening." Jamis said on her message device.

Kerra had heard the message but was very busy and thought to answer it later. When later did not happened; Jamis showed up and ordered everyone out of the lab. Kerra had rarely seen Jamis use his authority openly and was instantly concerned.

"What has happened father?" Kerra asked.

The speaker sat and looked at Kerra with sad eyes and a heavy heart.

"Were you aware that Brigand Sawyer's body is gone and his tomb has been ripped apart?" Jamis asked.

"What? This is an outrage!" Kerra yelled.

Jamis held up a hand to forestall anymore of Kerra's tirade. "There is more. It is believed that it was Brig himself that blew the tomb open and is now wondering around Grot like a mindless beast." Jamis explained.

"Is this possible father? Can Brig have been reanimated?" Kerra asked.

The speaker sat down by the window and seemed to reflect inward for several minutes. When he finally spoke he still did not look at Kerra, he just began.

"How much do you know about me, Kerra?" Jamis asked.

Kerra smiled at her father, the question seemed innocent and silly at the same time. She was going to say something flip when Jamis looked at her and she knew she really did not know the answer to his question. Jamis must have seen the realization in her eyes because he automatically began to explain.

"Kerra, I am the oldest living Kylr in the universe. In truth there is no Kylr even half my age. You are my natural daughter and you are quite brilliant in everyway. However, I am superior to you in everyway, I am also immortal. I look older than most Kylr, because I was an old man when I made the change to immortality. Your mother was the second person I changed; she did not wish to live forever but did not want to be without me either so she gave in. I did not change her like I did myself, so her life was merely extended not permanent.

"How did you do this father, how did you become the oldest Kylr, how do you continue when my mother died of old age?" Kerra asked.

(Sad Chuckle.)

"I am very special Kerra. Do you remember the story of how we drove the Grot horde from Kyl and later made friends with them?" Jamis asked.

"Yes of-course everyone knows the fairy tale, what of it?" Kerra asked a little perturbed.

Kerra's father looked at her with humorous eyes, like he was enjoying a private joke. It made Kerra angry that he was laughing at her. Kerra was in her eyes the smartest person alive, but her father always made her feel ignorant and less than.

"Fairy tale, how amusing; it all happened, every bit of it Kerra." Jamis said.

"How can you know that, that was nearly eight hundred years ago, in the time of Elor the first?" Kerra inquired.

"I know daughter…because it was I who drove the Grot from Kyl and made sure they never came back." Jamis said.

The look on Kerra's face was priceless. She was apoplectic, and shaking with uncontrolled emotions. Kerra fought herself to regain her footing.

"What?" Kerra asked.

"Oh don't play stupid Kerra it is beneath you." Jamis retorted sharply. "I need your mind sharp and open, if you are going to help me save the galaxy Kerra."

"Fine, you explain how this is possible and I will help you in any way I possibly can?" Kerra said.

Jamis smiled.

"I was an inventor years ago. I created the most important piece of technology the universe has ever seen. Can you guess what that is?" Jamis asked.

"The G-jen?" Kerra ventured.

"Yes, I created the G-jen. I was the very first Guardian of Kyl." Jamis told her.

"How can that be, you wear no G-jen; and to remove it once it is placed on your body is death?" Kerra asked

"Not in my case child. My G-jen is different from all the others I ever created. I was change while still alive, I do not have to wear my G-jen to use the power, I am a walking G-jen, and I have all the power without wearing the gauntlet." Jamis said.

"MY God father, I never knew. Wait, why do the other G-jen kill the user to place and remove it?" Kerra asked.

"A wise safety feature Kerra. If a rouge Guardian were to use his G-jen to do harm or evil they must be able to be stopped. Therefore, with that in mind I changed the G-jen to make it less powerful than mine and stoppable just incase. However, there are two more G-jen like my own. Can you guess who has those?" Jamis asked.

"I am guessing Brigand Sawyer was given the removable type. As to the other I would guess Jar." Kerra said.

"Jar, most definitely not; he is unworthy. Brigand does have the

removable type and he does not know it. There is more, out of
the three, there is no one stronger than the rest, and it is will
power that makes them so powerful. These three G-jen are
thousands of times stronger than the other G-jen." Jamis
explained.

"Then you must find and destroy Brig." Kerra said.

"It is not that simple daughter. The third G-jen was granted to
one of my own blood line...Korin." Jamis said calmly.

"Korin? She is a test tube baby father." Kerra said.

"She is also yours and Jar's daughter. It matters not that she was
not grown inside of you; she is still my granddaughter and a
powerful one at that. She now commands the entire Guardian
corps. The danger is this; Korin loves Brigand Sawyer, and if he
is lost then she might not be able to destroy him. Other than
myself; Korin is the only one capable of destroying Brigand, and
that will only be if he can't use the power of his gauntlet to
defend himself." Jamis said.

"The only hope of the universe is in Korin's tiny hands. I love her
you know, Jar hates her, but I am prouder of her than any of my
other children. Korin will do what must be done, she is the
strongest person I know...next to you father." Kerra said.

"I think the universe of Korin, she will do what is right, and so
will Jillian in the end. However, if anyone gets in their way,
Jillian with her Glave and Korin with a golden G-jen...well survival
would be iffy at best." Jamis said.

The doctor in Kerra began to contemplate how to treat or stop
the unstoppable for the greater good of the Kylr and the galaxy.
Kerra looked at Jamis and smiled. Kerra was a genius, and she
just flexed her brain and found a good idea.

"We cannot hope to defeat Brig G-jen or not, that man has more metal in his spine than any other person I have ever known. Korin is also of his ilk, and unbelievably Jillian has become the fiercest non Guardian warrior in the Galaxy. We clearly cannot attack these people and hope to prevail, so with that said; here is my advice. We seek out Brig's body and use the Snakoid healing fluid to try to restore him to the Brig we knew, if that fails, we used the poison to kill him or keep him near death and harmlessly in a coma." Kerra stated.

The Kylr man listened to Kerra and thought is was a logical course of action. Force was not an option, unless they wanted to fight Jillian, Korin, and a few other powerful Guardians. Guile on the other hand was the best option.

"We will need Matho and his assassin skills if we are to get close enough to stop Brigand Sawyer. It was Brig after all who taught the Pirz youth to snipe an enemy." Jamis explained.

"Father, I think we should keep this operation to our own people." Kerra said.

"No, Brig is a hero to our people and they might not do what has to be done, Matho on the other hand is all business and will help out because he would know Brig does not want to live as an undead monster." Jamis explained.

(ON THE PLANET PIRZ)

Mart was in counsel waiting for Matho to make his report. The younger Pirz had become the law, in mind and body. All the Pirz loved both Mart and Matho, for they were just; in all things. Matho had been injured rooting out some smugglers that set up a base on the far side of Pirz. Matho had refused to take time off of his duties for what he called a small injury. The injury was not so small and it was very serious, however, Matho was as tough as nails and nobody wanted to challenge him over it.

"Matho, welcome to the counsel. What is your report on the smugglers situation?" Mart asked.

The counsel was made up of men and women, poor and rich, old and young. Among the members, Matho was held in the highest esteem. When the law keeper spoke all listened and noted what he said as if it were the most important news ever. Matho was a young man of few words and great deeds.

"We found that there were aliens trespassing on Pirz soil, worse they were using our people as slave labor. It was brought to my notice by a farmer who traded goods out in that region. The farmer snuck into the town and watched for two long days, while avoiding capture to make sure he had something to tell me other than there was trouble. His intelligence was near perfection, we were out numbered and out gunned, but they were not prepared for us or the level of combat we were used to. In the end we captured thirteen criminals, and lost one Pirz to a mortal wound." Matho reported.

Large Marge who was Matho's field commander when he was in counsel usually came with him this time. Marge was seven feet tall and three hundred pounds. She wore custom body armor made by Rok, the giant Kyl Guardian. Marge was as fast as a pit viper and all muscle. She had a single scar on her face, but Marge was still beautiful to look at. She loved Matho, and God help anyone who crossed Matho or sought his life, Marge would just kill them. Marge was not a nice person as such; she was as silent as space. Matho was a small young man, but he had deep feelings for his giant female friend and she was the only person he trusted with his life.

"Matho was nearly killed retrieving the hostages; he is as usual a hero." Marge said with respect.

"I am well enough despite Marge's brooding." Matho said.

"I have heard reports that back up Officer Marge's statements my friend. You must remember you are not replaceable Matho, the Pirz people are under your protection and judgment, please do not risk your neck for no reason." Mart said.

"I can't send another into harms way while I stay safe, this is not the way I was trained. It is not the way of a commander or a man." Matho said firmly.

"Yes, I know. You are not Brigand Sawyer though, he could take a lot of damage and live because his gauntlet healed him." Mart said.

(LAUGHTER)

"Mart you have no idea what made Brig tick. Did you know he was already dead before he came to our planet? It was not the G-jen that made him live, it was his will to live and his focus on his duty, he simply refused to die before he saved us from the tyrants that ruled this planet, and stop a war?" Matho said.

"What do you mean dead before he came/" Mart asked.

"Brig was saturated with Snakoid poison, when he saved his friend from many bites; he boiled the Wira and himself to the point of death to cleanse the wounds. Oru who is the Wira survived, but even with his G-jen the poison killed him. He was in so much pain that all other injuries were like fly nips to him. His last act of bravery was done after he left. He placed himself in the star drive to get his friends and crew home. His body was buried on Grot." Matho said with regret.

The chamber door opened and a courier ran in and stopped out of breath. Mart looked at him, as did everyone else. Marge had her pulse rifle trained on him, just incase. She was always alert and ready to defend. The man final caught his breath and stood up straight cleared his throat and spoke.

"Speaker Jamis of the Kylr is on his way here for Matho the law bringer, he called ahead to be sure he would not be a surprise to our people." The man said.

"Speaker Jamis is coming here? We must not look like a race armed for war when he arrives, it would be a terrible insult." Mart said.

"Wrong answer Mart, we must do exactly the opposite, Jamis sent Guardians here to stop a war, and they did that; plus they freed our people. We must give the speaker a full military welcome and security detail. His safety must not be in jeopardy at any time." Matho said.

"Margy, see to it girl." Matho ordered gently.

"I am on it Matho, trust me to make all the preparations." Marge said.

The giant left the room easily dragging the courier with her. When she left and the door closed, both Mart and Matho spoke.

"Margy?" Mart asked.

"Yes Margy, we are close. I am not sure why she decided to watch over me, but I am extremely lucky she did. Marge is second to none in combat, and she can shoot as well as myself. I am the only person she has ever let close to her because of her unusual size and strength. I find her very pleasant to be with and a damn fine officer. If I should be killed Marge will take my place as chief law bringer." Matho said.

"I find no objection to that request; Marge is respected by all the Pirz. Now, about the speaker Jamis, why would he come here? Do you believe he will bring Guardians with him?" Mart asked.

"I hope he does. Since we have had smugglers down here on our planet; that means they are operating elsewhere as well, the Guardians need to know this." Matho explained.

"Once again Matho; you show that your judgment is sound." Mart said.

    The counsel broke up and went separate ways. Matho went to the Law Center. Mart made his way to the kitchen of the capitol to make sure Jamis had a good meal during his visit.

CHAPTER 9: THE TASK

It was early morning when Jamis was alerted that they were in Pirz space. Jamis looked out the porthole and noticed there were still pieces of ripped up ships in the space between the moons and the planet.

"My God what a battle Milo pitched out here. No wonder Brigand and the other Guardians field promoted the man to captain." Jamis thought.

The Kyl ship circled the planet and then made contact with the center government and asked for permission for Jamis and his personal guards to come to the planet. The Pirz space forces sent to two war ships to meet and escort Jamis to the proper landing pad in the city since there were many to choose from. The captain of the Kyl ship had its shields raised and guns brought to bear on both ships.

"No skipper, they mean us no harm. They are truly here to escort us, for safety sake. They are being intelligent about this, I am important to the Kylr people and they would be put off if I were harmed." Jamis chuckled.

On the ground twenty minutes later, in the appointed landing area; the Pirz law bringers were standing by. Jamis disembarked from his ship with two young Guardians, Rob and Dirk who were steely eyed twins. Rob is the laid back talker, and Dirk is the serious enforcer type, together they are the best Guardians of Kyl that the academy has graduated in a long time. They were perfectly balanced as a team. Korin wanted them to be assigned to her, but Jamis asked for them, prior to Korin leaving on a mission. Jamis had high hopes for these boys.

"Mr. Speaker of Kyl, we are here to escort you to the counsel building and a welcome meal" Marge told them.

"I require an immediate audience with the man known as Matho." Jamis said calmly.

Marge is not one to easily be put off; she smiled and continued on with her mission.

"I can arrange that after your meal sir if you wish." Marge said.

Jamis smiled, but the twins did not.

"Let me put it another way young lady. I require only a meeting with Matho, and do not wish to dine at all. The matter is of an urgent nature, so please take me to Matho presently?" Jamis explained.

"I am under orders to see to your safety and deliver you in that state to the dining hall sir, please just come long." Marge said.

"She is a bit thick, isn't she?" Dirk said.

"Yah, but she is kind of hot for a tall chick." Rob answered.

"Boys watch your manners." Jamis warned.

Neither of the twin had any delusion about who was stronger in their wee group and they followed Jamis by choice, like he was their own grandfather. They felt a unique honor by just being chosen to assist Jamis; and that is all they were doing assisting him.

"Matho is two hundred yards that way." Dirk said.

"Shall I fetch him for you Jamis?" Rob asked.

Marge looked at Jamis as if he had two heads. The honored speaker, who was to be the guess of Mart; had no intention of playing along, even though she was pleasant to him. Jamis looked at Rob.

"Time is against us son, please bring the young man to me...unharmed. One other thing; he was trained by Brig and Korin so he is likely dangerous, be nice." Jamis advised.

Rob turned into a blue missile and shot over the buildings into the city. Marge whipped her rifle up to shot him down, but Dirk shattered it with a quick left hand chop. Dirk smiled at her and began to glow like blue flames, he did not speak.

A half mile away Matho was getting ready for his visit with Jamis; he was currently something he never was; namely late. Matho heard soft feet walk up to his door and had not the person knocked Matho would have sent a volley through the door. Matho with his pistol in his hand walked to the door and opened it. Standing in the door was a young man about his own age. Matho gave him a fast combat scan and knew he was a Guardian of Kyl. The man was smiling at him at first and then he scowled. Before Matho could do anything he was being carried into his own house over the man's shoulder.

"Jesus, Mary and Joseph; you are all messed up pal. What were you going for martyr; you have a stab and projectile wounds." Rob said.

Rob went to work on the injured parts of Matho's body. Matho had seen Brig do this when he was here so he held still. Rob pulled a vial of yellow sweet smelling fluid and opened it.

"Put out your tongue buddy, don't worry it tastes good as well, like fruit." Rob explained.

Matho did as he was told and the liquid was tasty in its own way. Matho almost immediately felt great as the single drop of fluid was absorbed into his system.

"What was that?" Matho asked.

"I will tell you later, now might not be the best time. Jamis needs you healthy and ready to go." Rob said fast.

Matho was a good solider and he knew when to let others do their job as well. So he did not complain when Rob healed him with his G-jen and gave him a healing potion. Matho also did not complain when Rob pulled him out the door and launched them both into the air. That little trick was originated by Brig. The short flight or blast off and fall to the ground took very little time. Matho was set down firmly in font of Marge who was red faced with anger.

"Are you okay Matho?" Marge asked.

"Yes, I have nothing to fear from the Guardians of Kyl." Matho said. "Or do I?"

The Guardians smiled and Jamis did as well. The speaker walked forward and held out his hand. Matho smiled and shook it.

"I am told great things about you Matho, my senior Guardians think extremely highly of your abilities. I have come on a matter of desperate importance; that I believe only you are uniquely suited to help me with. Will you hear me out and then make a decision?" Jamis asked.

"I'm hungry Jamis." Matho said.

The law bringer turned and walked off toward the capitol building and the dinner that was planned. Jamis smiled at the younger man's willful tact. Marge was ordered to bring them to eat and so Matho was making sure that happened.

The hall was well lighted and the food was glorious both in smell and in taste. Mart was a great host and funny chatterbox once he had a wee little bit of spirits. Large Marge stood not sat by Matho in a most protective way, Jamis could see the Amazon girl loved the young man plain as day. Matho seemed to feel at the least similar affection for her, despite their size difference. Matho would never have struck anyone as helpless; his eyes marked him as a slayer. Jamis noticed that Matho was looking at him in a curious way. The time had come; the man was ready to hear his news and request now.

"Mart I had a great time this evening, you are a fine and generous host." Matho said.

"Why thank you Matho." Mart said in a tipsy voice.

"Sadly, I have duties that will take me away from this party and into counsel with Speaker Jamis." Matho explained.

That did it for Mart, his tipsy act was over instantly. He turned and spoke to the steward who was in charge of the dinner and the lady shook her head.

"To all my guests; thank you for coming, and you have all been a joy. I must attend to urgent matters with the law bringer and Speaker Jamis now, so please excuse me." Mart said.

Mart got up when Matho did, he followed Marge out the doors

into the hallway that lead to the private offices. Marge tapped the wall pad by one of the door and the door opened to a pair of rifle barrels. Marge said a few phrases and the guns were lowered and the lawmen came out and took up posts beside the door as Marge invited the group into the room.

"This room is private and secure." Marge said.

"We will see?" Dirk stated roughly.

The tall handsome Guardian held up his hand and the room was bathed in soft blue light. One red dot appeared. Marge was about to react but Rob snickered. The other twin had a laser pointer and was messing with his brother. Dirk only smiled for Rob, and he did so now.

"Good one brother." Dirk said. "The room is secure, well done Marge."

Marge was not used to having anyone other than Matho praise her, and Dirk was being sincere so it made feel all the more embarrassed.

"Marge it is a rare thing for my brother to say anything nice, so it is deep respect my brother offers you; that is no small thing. You have, by your actions since we landed, proven yourself worthy of our friendship." Rob explained.

"Thank you...both." Marge said.

There was a round table in the room with four chairs. Only three were used. Marge and the twins stood back against the walls and let Jamis, Matho and Mart converse alone.

"Why have you come?" Mart asked.

Jamis lost his smile and the deep look of concern replaced it. Mart must have thought he had offended the speaker because he sat back shocked. Matho reached back and held Marge's hand, so that she would see he was relaxed. The twin's made no reaction at all.

"We have a problem." Jamis said.

"The Kylr?" Mart asked.

"The galaxy, Mart, has a problem." Jamis said.

The room went silent for forty-five minutes while the speaker of the Kylr explained everything; right up to the point where they sat down to eat dinner. Matho never blinked once he learned Brig was not laid out in a tomb. Matho had the look of a deadly predator suddenly.

"Just so there is no misunderstand; Jamis, please tell me why you sought me out? I have my own theory, but I would like to hear yours?" Matho said.

Jamis smiled and so did the twins.

"Brig told Rok you were the finest combat mind he met on Pirz, a natural leader he said; it is plain to see he was spot on about you." Rob commented.

Dirk nodded his agreement, being a man of action not words.

"I have come to ask you to hunt down the body of Brigand Sawyer and decide if he can be saved, or kill him if he cannot be saved. If he is a mindless, soulless creature do not let the memories of the Brig you used to know stop you from stopping him. This is the final option of-course, we want to save him at all costs but if we can't then..." Jamis said sadly

All eyes were on Matho. Mart thought he would refuse. Marge was scared he would accept, it was a suicide mission to hunt a Guardian.

"When do we leave? I want at least one Guardian left here to protect my world in my absence. Can you arrange that?" Matho asked.

"We will stay in your place as long as Master Jamis does not object." Rob offered.

"I brought you for this purpose; however I too have a request. Mart must allow you to literally take Matho's place in his absence, as a law giver and a counsel member, until he returns. I do not ask for pride or for spying purposes but for safety and sacred trust. I will give my word this world will go unharmed for as long as Matho is gone, that will take cooperation." Jamis explained.

Mart looked shocked at the request, Kylr or not; this was a grave request. It was a no brainer though, two Guardians looking after Pirz.

"It would be my pleasure to have you fine young men helping us out while Matho is away. You can help Marge lead the law bringers." Mart said.

"Hold your tongue fool! It is not up to you who runs the law bringers, it is up to Matho, you have no authority over us; remember that!" Marge said forcefully.

Mart was shocked and nervous, Marge was not known for forgiveness and he had just over stepped his authority. He was going to speak again but Matho spoke for him.

"He did not mean any disrespect Margy, it was a friendly suggestion and a good one. The Guardians can help make sure that those smugglers don't get a toe hold on us while we are still weakened by the last war. Help them to help us...please?" Matho said.

The tall yet pretty girl let a few tears fall on Matho's face. Matho took her hand and turned to look at the Speaker.

"Two hours from now at your ship, I will be there ready to go. But not until then, I wish to be left alone." Matho looked at Mart.

The lawman left the room, towing Marge behind him. Wisely nobody spoke or moved from the room as they left. Matho took Marge away because she was going to cry and he did not want her to be embarrassed by it. Matho need not have bothered, Marge could care less what anyone but Matho thought. Her tears were for him.

Matho towed Marge back toward his home, but she stopped him and turned him toward hers. Matho opened her door and lead her in. Marge put her pulse rifle down by the door and pulled Matho into her bedroom. She wanted to say something, but could not. Matho took a breath and started unbuckling her body armor. Marge let him. When he was done he slipped out of his own armor and arms and pulled the covers back on her long bed and pushed her towards the bed, she went and laid down, and Matho scooted in beside her. She put her head on his chest. He ran his hand through her soft slightly curly hair.

"I just want to hold you in my arms before I go and I want to make you a promise Margy. When I return I would like you to consider marrying me, don't answer me yet, just think about it; because I love you. You are the only woman for me, I might be a small fellow but, I feel like I can do anything when you're with me." Matho told her.

(SOB)

"I am afraid you won't come back Matho and my life will become an empty void of duty. You are the only joy I have ever known, first as a friend and then more over time. I want to go with you, but I have to look after Pirz; if you cannot be here to do it" Marge said with tears running freely down her cheeks.

"Don't cry Margy, if Brig can live through dying and come back for his love, then I can as well. Nothing could make me not come back to you; nothing at all." Matho said.

Marge would have spoken but Matho stopped her by kissing her on the lips passionately. Marge gave in and they held each other in a warm embrace for the entire two hours.

CHAPTER 10: MERCS

The missing mercenaries caught the attention of the Grot patrols. The fact that the loud mouthed Mercs did not check in or come back when they were called to report after a week or so; left the Grot security patrol no choice but to look for the distasteful weaklings. It was only by chance that they found them. If it had not been raining for two days hard and heavy, the Grot would not have found the bodies buried in the dirt. Their bodies were scooped up out of the ground and took back to the Capitol for analysis. The bodies were cut up and the bones were snapped.

Elon looked the bodies over briefly with Rok at his side. The crown prince thought it was a good idea to search the surrounding area for more clues to what happened to the Mercs. Rok did not object to this suggestion. Two days later the patrol found a Grim'oc with lethal wounds; dead in the brush along the predator's tree line hunting grounds. The Grim'oc as a predator were pretty deadly, even the Grot had to be careful when they were on foot in the wilds to not meet one unprepared.

"These wounds were made by an expert killer. Look at the pattern of the strikes; they are all in lethal areas, or in a crippling manner." Rok observed

The Grot prince did indeed see what the giant Guardian was saying. He was a skilled hunter and killer. There was not animal who could make the wounds, they were very skilled by the look.

"This was not Brigand Sawyer; the wounds were not made by a G-jen. They were made by a blade of some sort." Elon said.

"I agree, so it is important to let your patrols know that there is a dangerous being out there of immense strength and skill. The Grim'oc is a huge beast and deadly killer, yet it is the one dead and there is no other creature lying dead out there; therefore, it is still out there." Rok said.

Elon and Rok had made their peace and actually liked each other. They were two huge powerful fighters, and they had a strict code of right and wrong that they shared. Only race separated them. Rok let Bello know what they discovered while he was on his way to the port to meet Jamis; that was coming not from Kyl but from Pirz, which confused Rok.

Korin was not happy to hear about the dead super predator that was killed by a better killer. The fact it was not Brig or at least done by a G-jen made her less than happy. Oru however had a different opinion. The Wira monkey in giant Wolf-tiger-ape form turned and went like the wind into the wilds where the Grim'oc was found. In practically no time at all Oru had found the place the Grim'oc was killed. Oru circled and sniffed with his sharp Wolf-tiger senses. He stopped and spoke.

"Jilly and Korin walk for meenit, streech leegs now." Oru said in a kind tone.

The girls slid off Oru's back and realized they were a tad bit saddle sore. That was not why Oru had them get off. Oru could tell they were about to be attacked and by something big.

(CRASH...SNAP)

The brush and tree limps were trampled and broken as a huge beast ripped into Oru. Korin was already glowing Bright green when she tried to step in front of Jillian to protect her. Korin was nearly cut down when Jillian instantly snapped the Glave to life.

Oru was knocked rolling, but he was on his feet in attack position instantly. The Beast was a Grim'oc female; which are larger than the males and more deadly. Oru was not in the mood for this crap right now; and he had four huge powerful ape arms that the Grim'oc did not. Oru reached out in a flash and grabbed the Grim'oc by the nape of its neck and tossed it sprawling into a big tree trunk. The beast was stunned by Oru's power and snarled but backed wisely away and burst into the trees and was gone.

"Oru no play with beasty, need to find Breeg!" Oru said in his broken way.

Korin looked at Jillian who raised her brow at Oru.

"Guess our little friend is serious today." Jillian said.

"No doubt about it, Oru means business. He is clear minded about his goal and will not let anything interrupt that goal." Korin said.

"No, Oru die; much pain now. Find my Breeg or no die!" Oru said as he looked at the girls.

It was true, Oru had the signs of great pain and strain in his giant eyes. Moreover, there was something else there as well; Determination and loyalty. Oru meant what he said, and he would not die not matter what until Brig was saved or laid to rest.

"Breeg here, he fight big beasty, Brig hurt, but beasty die. More bigger beasty not fight Brig, they go that wee." Oru said pointing to a spot in the valley.

"There was a second beast Brig did not fight? Why didn't Brig just use his G-jen to kill the Grim'oc; and why would he go off in to the wild lands instead of coming home to us?" Korin rasped as tears welled up in her eyes.

Jillian squeezed Korin's arm and Korin looked into Jillian's hard blue eyes and saw something she did not know was there. Jillian had changed, she was tougher than most Guardians now and the look of deep resolve matched Oru's pledge to find Brig.

"He may not remember us Korin. We WILL make him remember us and then we are going to take our man home with us. God help anyone who tries to prevent us from our objective." Jillian told her mate.

Two gigantic ape hands snatched the girls off the ground and deposited them on Oru's back. The girls did not fight the lift. Oru took a deep sniff of the area and the air.

"We go now." Oru said as he burst to speed in the direction of the scent of his bond mate.

(ELSEWHERE IN THE WILDS)

Tigra was very unhappy about leaving her new friend. He was a strange being; he had an odd power about him for a small frail looking person. His hands were rough from toil, but gentle when he touched her. Tigra had always shunned sex and emotions as useless, but this man made her feel more alive in a few hours than she had in her entire hard life. Tigra was re-evaluating her lifestyle and chosen path; perhaps she had been wrong to shut the universe out and go it alone. Alone was no longer her desired state. However, until she found the body of the hero, she must remain alone and follow through with her job.

"I will be back my new friend and then I will not let anything separate us again." Tigra said to herself out loud.

The skilled hunter moved silently through the countryside in search of either the body of a hero or the scum who took it.

(IN A TREE WATCHING THE TAROCS)

The alien saw the bounty hunters attacking the Tarocs and was going to off them, but he hesitated for some unknown reason. A moment later a group of huge powerfully built, well armed warriors came into view. They pulled down on the bounty hunters and fired. The transports the hunters were using were now fodder, shot to pieces by the new aliens. Tarc went out and spoke to the large creatures with the heavy arms and a few moments later Tarc had killed all three of the hunters. The Huge bipedal creature said he was looking for an alien and Tarc called the big warrior a Grot.

"Grot?" The tiny alien said.

The tiny alien watched the Grot leave carrying the bodies of dead bounty hunters; then he watched the Tarocs for a short while before deciding that once the sun went down over the purple and orange landscape he would say his farewell to Tarc. The herd was mostly asleep when the tiny alien slipped in to the circle and walked up to Tarc who was not sleeping, and not surprised to see his friend.

"Hello small one." Tarc said pleasantly.

"Hello Tarc and thanks." The tiny fellow said.

"Thanks...for what are you thankful?" Tarc asked.

"The Grot asked you about a dead hero and about any aliens you may have seen; you told him nothing when they are clearly looking for me. I am not dead, so I must be one of the bad guys, even though I can't recall a damned thing before walking and meeting you." The tiny alien said.

"Tiny you are my friend, you have fought for our herd and risked your life for me personally, and I would never give you up to those butchers the Grot." Tarc explained.

"Nevertheless Tarc, Mercs will keep coming to find me, and so will the Grot. Sooner than later they will decide to kill some of you just because, or maybe for food even though they are not hungry. I will no longer risk your lives to cover for me; I am leaving you tonight Tarc." Tiny said.

"Tiny one, you will be missed; and we will never aid anyone looking for you. You have been a good friend and companion to us. You are the first meat eating alien who did not try to kill us; rather you chose to repel your own nature for our benefit. You are not a villain or a bad man; it is not within you Tiny, it just simply is not in your nature." Tarc said.

Tarc knew Tiny was correct in leaving the herd, but he was the massive bovine's friend and that stirred him against his better judgment. Tiny sat with Tarc in silence for a few quiet hours. Tiny got up patted his friend on the shoulder and walked away into the night. Tiny kept walking right through dawn and mid morning; he never slowed down even when he saw Mercs coming his way.

Tiny only stopped once and that was to lead a patrol of Grot away from the Tarocs.

(IN THE PALACE WAR ROOM)

Matho was being brought up to speed on the situation. Matho wanted to see the Grim'oc and dead Mercs they found. The Grot captain showed him the bodies and Matho spent some time looking them over. While he was inspecting them Bello walked up to chat.

"Nobody is going to morn any of these creatures, but at least it was not Brig that killed them." Bello said.

"Wrong, Brig killed them all." Matho said.

Every face of every being in the room was agog instantly. Bello was about to say something haughty but Rok stalled him out.

"How do you figure that to be so, Matho?" Rok asked.

The Pirz assassin pulled a small double bladed blade and snapped his wrist. The blade flew across the room and stuck a fruit carrying it off the table and into the closest wall where it hung balancing.

"I am not a Guardian, so I do not rely on my G-jen to be the center of my logic, and I am no Grot who uses their muscles instead of their heads. Neither, was Brigand Sawyer. Brig could fight better empty handed than most warriors with all the weapons they could carry, he taught me to use everything as a weapon, but mostly to use my mind. It is true no energy weapon was used to kill any of these beings. Therefore they were killed by a warrior with extreme skill with a bladed weapon. The leaves out every single one of the Mercs, because at the time they were not here to kill the Grim'oc, and they don't kill their own, call that professional courtesy. It also leaves out the Grot, because the slashes are far too small and precise of a pattern for the large power race, and the cuts are not deep enough to suggest the powerful blows of a Grot warrior. Ipso facto that leaves our friend

Brig who is a master killer, and he taught me, but I am not up to his level" Matho explained in detail.

The room looked at the fruit pinned to the wall and then at the dead bodies. There was no longer doubt that Brig killed all of them.

"Damn it; that means Brig can still reason and think. If he were a mindless beast, he would be easy prey, but as a person who can work out tactics and a battle plan, we dare not hunt him with anything but the greatest caution." Bello admitted.

"I have come to bring in Brig...alive. I will work alone; if any of you interfere with me; then I will name you my enemy and act on that as needed, so stay away or risk death." Matho said.

The Guardians knew Matho, they served with him in the Pirz liberation war; this was not an idol threat. Matho was only second to Brig in close quarters combat, and he could shoot the eyes out of flying bugs. Matho was the law on an entire planet; this guy was tough and deadly. The Grot did not know it though and spoke like fools.

"Why do we listen to this tiny weakling?" The Grot warrior next to the captain said.

Before the Grot could continue he speech; there was a blade dipped in Snakoid poison protruding from his trachea. The Grot was on his knees dying an instant later. Matho just looked at him. The captain actually laughed out loud and so did the prince.

"Shall I save him Elon or is he to die a horrible death?" Matho asked.

Everyone knew what was on the blade by the way the Grot was dropped. They all looked at Matho like he was mad.

"Can this be done; is there a way to counter the poison?" Elon asked seriously.

Matho answered the question with actions not words. He walked over to the Grot and pulled the blade from his throat, simultaneously taking out a flask full of yellow liquid. Matho rubbed the yellow liquid all over the wound and then spoke.

"Open your mouth big guy." Matho ordered.

The Grot was still in insane pain; but he did as he was told. Matho put two drops on his tongue and told the Grot to swallow it. Matho sat on the table and watched. The Grot male got to his feet and looked Matho squarely in the eyes and smiled. Matho earn the respect of the entire Grot at that moment. Elon declared Matho a friend to the crown and a dangerous enemy in one move. What that meant is; no Grot would dare attack Matho, if they did and died; Matho would not be held responsible. The Grot are a very honorable race, they would never go back on a word given or back jump an ally.

"I want all the Mercs on Grot to be rounded up paid and sent off my world now." Elon ordered.

All but one mercy was accounted for by the end of the day, several were dead, and the rest were happy to get a fist full of gold or gems and leave Grot for good. Elon was not happy that the one hunter left unaccounted for was the best...Tigra.

CHAPTER 11: CATCH THE TIGER

Jillian was exhausted but she would never say that out loud. Jillian was never, not ever going to be the weak link again; so help her God. Korin was beyond spent and so was Oru; none of them would admit it however.

Just as Oru crested a hill, they all heard the sounds of animals grazing and milling around. Oru was starving and in his Wolf-tiger-ape form he was a meat eater. Oru leapt over the ridge and flattened a beast. It looked like a cow only monster sized with four horns and big intelligent eyes. Jillian dove off Oru's back and the Glave came to life, just as she was about to cut the cows head off; Oru yanked the beast out of range.

"NO Jilly, they smell like Breeg." Oru said in haste.

The entire herd of Tarocs stopped where they were when Oru saved their herd member. Tarc walked forward and looked at Oru carefully with quizzical eyes. The Tarocs were previously going to charge and trample the three hunters; they would have been killed if they had not stopped.

"Oru is sorry beasty, we are hungry and you smell good to starving seekers like we." Oru said.

"What is it that you seek?" Tarc asked.

Korin nearly fainted from shock as Tarc's rich tenor voice spoke from behind her.

"We search for our loved one." Jillian said.

"For what purpose?" Tarc asked.

"OMG!" Jillian exclaimed as everything turned a misty green.

Korin went off like a green neutron bomb; the energy waves coming over her turned the green-purple grass to ash. The Tarocs did not move, they seemed to understand this was a pivotal moment in the first meeting.

"OUR PURPOSE IS OUR OWN; YOU WILL TELL ME WHAT I WANT TO KNOW!" Korin screamed.

"Korin!" Jillian snapped.

The Guardian was more deeply disturbed by the loss of Brig than could be explained. Korin was a loner until Brig and Jillian invited her into their hearts and lives. When Brig died, in a way so did Korin. The hope of finding Brig alive in any form gave her back an intense hope of a brighter future that she had thought lost forever. Korin dropped the king's share of her deadly aura and simply glowed menacingly.

"We look for our Breeg, because we love him and he needs us. Jilly and Korin our Breeg's mates. I am bonded to Breeg. If Breeg has trouble then we help." Oru tried to explain.

Tarc walked not up to Jillian or Oru who seemed ready for a conversation, but up to Korin. The huge Tarocs looked her in the eyes and sighed.

"You have the same wild look in your eyes as Tiny does. He has a fire burning in his soul that nothing could ever put out. I think I understand you Kylr child. You are different from your people, are you not? Tiny and his mate accepted you and loved you like no other ever has, this changed you so that now you cannot go back to the void in your soul from before." Tarc said.

Korin's diamond pupils disappeared behind big oyster tears, she sobbed silently. Tarc was not finished, he had more to say.

"I am told by the Grot that Tiny is a hero. I know this to be true because he has protected my herd from threats both wild and domestic. He is sadly no longer with us." Tarc said.

"Where did he go?" Jillian asked.

"I really don't know, he left in the black of night. Tiny got up, touched my shoulder, smiled one last time and was gone." Tarc told them.

Tarc looked at the ground in a guilty way and Korin was about to jump him, but Oru put his massive hands around Korin and shook his head no and then nodded back at the huge bovine.

"I swore to Tiny I would not tell anyone about him, but I feel I must. Tiny does not know who he is; he simply can't remember anything before meeting my herd. He thinks he must be one of the grave robbers that stole the hero's body, but I know that he is the hero; they call Brigand Sawyer." Tarc said.

"What, then why didn't you tell him to go back and make contact?" Jillian asked with angry tears in her eyes.

"No, that would be bad. The Guardians think Brig is soulless and they will attack him without pause. The Grot will do the same because of how powerful Brig is, they can't take a chance that he is a rouge. Brig must not go back until we find him and figure out whether he is safe or not." Korin said.

Oru sniffed the air and the ground and wondered around for a few minutes while Jillian and Korin chatted with Tarc.

"Tiny is not a danger to anyone who does not attack him or someone he cares about. He has a sense of justice that is part of his personality; that is showing through. He sat many nights just looking at the stars. He said they looked wrong to him many times." Tarc said.

"Brig is not from this galaxy. He came from a planet called Earth. I am from there as well. We have been together since we were small children and he was always my hero. I guess some things never change. I want to find him and help him remember, because life without Brig is no life at all to me." Jillian explained.

"You are not a Guardian?" Tarc inquired.

"No she is not, but she is the mistress of the Glave, which means she is nearly as powerful as a Guardian. Wait, why doesn't Brig use his G-jen?" Korin asked.

"Tiny is a Guardian?' Tarc asked.

"Yes, did you not see the G-jen on his left arm?" Korin asked.

"No, his arms were always wrapped in cloth or hides. I thought it was to protect his arms while he fought so fiercely. I now believe he thought is was a sign of slavery or that he was a prisoner of some kind; he covered it in shame." Tarc said.

Korin sat on a big rock and looked at the stars and then she scanned the land until she found Oru. He was shaking, The Wira was dying a horrible death, his insides were trying to revert to something but it could not because he was two creatures combined. Poor Oru so dedicated to Brig and his little family. Korin vowed to find a way to save Oru. Korin looked at Jillian;

who was also watching Oru, she looked sick with concern. Jillian had changed, she had become strong and fierce; however, her tender heart and kindness remained.

"Brig does not know how to use the G-jen, and that gives us a better chance to catch him and talk things through." Korin said to Jillian.

"Not much though, Brig is a hunter / tracker who will fight until there is nothing left of him if pressed. He was already extremely dangerous before he was a Guardian, now he may be the most dangerous person alive. We must approach him with caution and love or he will fight or flee." Jillian explained.

Oru walked up and plopped down.

"Oru is hungry and thirsty." Oru muffled out his mouth.

"A short way down the tree-line there are fruits and a clean water source. We avoid it because there is almost always a Grim'oc waiting to pounce on us, but I assume that is not a problem for you three?" A smaller Tarocs said

"Do you like the fruiters little four horn?" Oru asked in his broken way.

The smaller Tarocs walked closer and rubbed her face on his neck.

"You smell like a friend to me, so I will show you where the fruits are if you keep the killer from hurting me. Yes, I like the fruits very much; it is not safe for us little ones to get to close to them though." The female Tarocs said.

"Oru will protect you. What is your name?" Oru asked.

"I have none." The Tarocs said.

'We will call you Tora then, if you don't mind?" Jillian said.

    Tora looked at Tarc as the leader of the herd, he was the law.
He shook his head at her. She smiled at him and turned back to
Jillian and Oru.

"I would be honored to go by that name." Tora said excited.

    Tora lead the trio down to the fruit tree lane and the water
source. Oru stopped them before they got to close to the trees
and sniffed the air. The Oru monster looked at Korin. She shook
her head and disappeared in the trees. Oru went in at another
angle. A moment later there was crashing and slamming noises.
It was quite a din. It all ended with a green blast and the smell of
freshly cooked meat. Oru came out of the woods covered in
blood, Korin was behind him limping.

"There were three of them in there, we only saw two. Number
three was older and big. It was lying in the weeds to pick us off,
Oru saved me from a lot more damage, and he is hurt pretty bad."
Korin said.

"Oru is fine, very much need food. No eat the yucky beasty, they
are not good." Oru said.

    Tora and Tarc followed Oru to the fruit trees while Jillian
snapped the Glave to life and guarded the group while they ate
the delicious fruits. The rest of the herd crowded around and ate
their fill of the great fruit. No other Grim'oc or predator came
near the grove of trees. Oru told Jillian he would know before
they even got close. Jillian knew this to be true, but she still
watched carefully all the more because her friends just fought a
battle.

(IN THE HILLS)

Tigra was roaming the hills. She saw a few smugglers and laughed to herself that the Grot would have kittens if they knew there were pirate and smuggling operation on their own planet. All the strength in the world will not stop what you don't know about. The Grot were a very arrogant race, their power base was only second to the Kylr it was commonly believed. Tigra did not hold to this belief, her on people the Karna were the greatest hunters in the universe; they can kill an enemy with little effort due to their speed and agility. Only the Kylr can resist their might, the Grot would be slaughtered. The Karna used whatever weapon it took to win, the Grot had a false sense of honor that would not let them take advantage of an opponent, and the Karna would just kill you. It rankled Tigra's fur that her alien friend took her so easy and unaware.

There was a green flash in the valley in a dark tree lined area; it caught Tigra's sharp eyes. She pulled out her binoscope and zeroed in on the area. There was a herd of Bovines, a Kylr female, the biggest monster Tigra had ever seen and a...

"What...she looks like my alien. She is one of them. My alien was a robber." Tigra said in outrage to herself.

Tigra was mad at herself for letting her emotions get in the way of her judgment. This is why she never had relationships, because they got in her way. Tigra vowed to hunt down the alien and kill him for this. Once again the Karna hunter let her emotions and pride out weight her common sense. Her alien was good to her and she forgot this in her blind anger.

(IN THE FOOT HILLS NEAR THE MOUNTAINS)

The alien who the Tarocs call Tiny and who was born on a little blue marble in space, was confused and lost. Lost on Grot. The stars were just peeking out of the dark velvet cover as night rushed forward. Tiny stopped and made a small cold camp. He leaned back against the rocks and watched the stars. There was a memory tickling his mind about a red haired girl with the softest lips and her little gentle hands than held his rough ones so lovingly. The memory brought with it a stab of pain as he saw other men hurt her. The girl's blood was all over him as he ran through the snow, yes snow; he remembered that. He had been so desperate to save her and he had a burning pain in his own chest. Tiny's hand went to his chest involuntarily.

"WHO AM I!" he screamed into the night, as tears ran freely on to his chest.

Miles away Oru's head jerked up and his head snapped around. He heard the scream so far away with his Wolf-tiger hearing. Jillian looked at Oru, Korin was still eating and healing herself with her G-jen.

"What is it Oru?" Jillian asked.

"Pain, Jilly; Breeg is crying." Oru said sadly.

Both of them looked at the hills. Unknown to them Tigra heard the cry as well and was already moving to find the owner, although she deep down knew it was him.

Tiny was lost in grief for a minute. He stopped when his hunter and combat sense kicked in and he realized how stupid his outburst had been. He grabbed his stuff and booked out of there just before Tigra lifted her binoscope to look at the place her had just been from above him. Her scope showed a heat signature, thus she knew she just missed her target. The Game was on, and she intended to win. Only one problem; he was as good as or better than she was at this game. Tigra being a Karna was faster than the alien and likely stronger. Tigra believed her senses were superior to his as well. The nagging issue for her was how did he beat her senses to capture her in the first place and why had he not killed her. Tigra had the influx of happy thoughts unbidden to her mind again.

"Okay alien, first I capture you then I question you, perhaps I will have to kill you?" Tigra said out loud.

The Karna super hunter took off through the rocks and down the side of the mountain, so sure footed a mountain goat could not have done better.

Meanwhile, Tiny booked out of that area and then looped back to see who was on his tail. He stayed up wind from the pursuer, just in case they had better senses than he did. A strange thing happened; Tiny smelled a familiar sweet smell. He ran to catch up to the smell, he caught sight of Tigra as she ripped into the rock below him and then into a copse of trees. Tiny ran with everything he had, but Tigra had been correct about the speed difference. If Tigra would have stopped he would have ran right into her grasp. Tigra however, did not stop. Tiny lost her in the trees and rocks where no track signs showed.

Oru told Jillian and Korin to get aboard his back. The trio said their goodbyes and sent the Tarocs back to the open plains where the Grim'oc would not attack them wisely.

The plains disappeared under Oru's Wolf-tiger paws, and the Wira picked up more speed as he went. Korin had never seen a living being that could match Oru's magnificent speed and grace. Yet, Korin and Jillian worried about him like mothers over a baby. Oru's insides were rebelling against his will power. His will power was winning...for now, but the cost was Oru's life.

"Why did you become something forbidden to just find Brig?" Korin asked.

"I could run fast and fight pretty good as a wolfy-cat, but might loose a fight and then no help Breeg. Or I could be big strong apey and win all fights, but no good to run. Breeg loose life first time for Oru, Oru give all for Breeg to pay back." Oru explained.

"Brig would be mad if he knew you were dying for him." Jillian said.

"No care if Breeg mad, only care if Breeg live." Oru said as he increased his speed again.

The miles to the mountains melted like butter under the power strides of Oru, is body was racked with spasms and Jillian could feel his heart being forced to obey, she wanted to cry; she did not because it would make Oru suffer more.

There were trees growing along the rocks less than a mile from where they were, Oru headed for them. Once they were in the shade of the trees Oru slowed to a walk as he smelled the area carefully. Just ahead of them there was movement, and then there was a plasma bolt that hit a tree and left a hole right through it. Jillian back flipped off of Oru's back; while pulled her Glave out. Korin took to the trees and surrounded herself and with a green corona that would repel any attack. Oru went invisible for the first time since he left KYL.

"Oh Shit!" Oru heard a voice say in the distance.

It was really to bad because so did Korin and she sent a hail storm of green energy flinging and it rocked into the area where the shot originated. The effect was like strafing a ground target from the air. Jillian was gone; Oru unseen, so Korin had to be careful not to injure her friends by mistake. Korin was peeved at their lack of coordination.

"Come" Oru said as an invisible hand grabbed Korin out of the tree.

Now that Korin knew where her giant friend was she could cut loose freely. Jillian was safe with the Glave in her hand; she can repel even Korin's force attacks. Where was she though?

There was a blur just behind Korin, a blast hit her corona and rocked her forward. The damn attacker was behind her already. They must be fast, really fast! Another hard blast hit Korin from the side this time. Korin saw that the attacker was moving fast off to her right side and that she did not see Jillian brandishing the Glave in her path because she was trying to score on Korin.

"Hello." Jillian said.

Jillian sent a right-cross into the attackers face. The attacker tried to hit Jillian with her small pulse rifle but Jillian was a master with the Glave and close quarters combat; so Jillian merely cut the rifle asunder in a blink of the attacker eyes. The attacker jumped back and pulled a dagger and renewed her attack. Jillian cut the dagger blade in three pieces with a flip of her wrist. The attacker was stunned but not beaten; they grabbed the pieces and threw them at Jillian. A gloved hand came up and knocked the middle one out of the air while the other two passed harmlessly Jillian.

"Good form miss, love to chat but I am hunting and it is not you I seek grave robber." Tigra said as she put on a burst of speed to put distance between herself and the trio.

Korin was going to blast Tigra but the Karna used the terrain to her benefit like a pro, which is exactly what she was. Even though they could not catch her yet the three followed her. Oru ran by Jillian who deftly grabbed Korin's hand and swung up on his back, so that Oru did not have to stop. Tigra however was not as far gone as they thought. She watched them in confusion. The Kylr was a Guardian and the girl carried what she believed to be the legendary Glave bladed sword. Impossible, that these three were the grave robbers. Tigra was very confused; she needed to find her alien and ask him about them without being captured or killed.

(ON TOP OF A RIDGE)

Tiny watched the small pitched battle and was intrigued by the red haired girl and the silver haired Manx that could shoot a green field around her. The girl with the red pony-tail carried a weapon like a sword, but it was much more and she was very good with it. Tiny made metal notes not to get two damn close to the red haired girl or in the open versus the silver haired female. Tiny wished that he got a look at their faces. More, what they hell was that giant thing that was invisible and then there again? Why did Tigra attack them? He had to catch up to her and ask her without getting himself killed; she was a Hired gun after all and a very good one at that.

CHAPTER 12: THE HILLS

Matho slipped out of the city alone. He had the sinking feeling that if he let anyone follow him, that his life or Brig's would be in jeopardy. Matho had a small pack on him. It contained food pellets that could sustain a man for a week with a single use. He had some extra clothing. He had medical supplies and lastly he carried weapons. His rifle was silent when fired. He had thirty small throwing blades, six close quarter daggers and two short swords for larger prey.

Bello watched Matho go standing beside Jamis. They knew Matho would leave alone and that he would not stop until his mission was complete or he was dead himself.

"Is it right sending a sheep to capture the ultimate wolf Jamis?" Bello asked the leader of his people.

"Perhaps not; however that young man from another world is the closest thing that we have to Brig's mental equal. They think alike and fight with a reckless abandon like no other men I have ever known. Matho is many times more likely to find Brig and deal with him one way or the other." Jamis said.

"What if Korin finds him out there? She will know that he was sent to take Brig down. Korin was one of the Guardians that helped trained Matho; she knows what he is and what he is capable of doing." Bello asked.

Jamis smiled at Bello and then continued to watch Matho trekking across the fields just on the edge of the city.

"Even mighty Korin has weakness and Matho is no easy target. He is also not rash or stupid; if Korin is in the area Matho will not cross her without having the higher ground." Jamis said.

Matho was half way across the plains before he stopped for rest. The young man knew enough to stay clear of the trees or even clusters of scrubs; that is where the predators were waiting to pick you off. The Grot were right in one way about Matho, he was not qualified to hunt down Brig...nobody was.

The day went by and the night fell and still Matho continued on. By the mid-day sun of the second day Matho was exhausted and there was no one around to watch or judge him, however, Matho would say to himself "Would fatigue stop Brig? No, nothing would stop Brig; not even death." Therefore, Matho continued on at an insane pace.

(HIGH ABOVE THE PLANET)

Milo was not happy about being sent to watch for sign of Brig. It seemed to him that he was considered a lower member of the team and useless to boot, so they sent him out on a lackey's mission to keep him out of the way. Milo was angry, and he was one of the people who serve and was shaped by his friendship with Brigand Sawyer as was his chief; so Milo decided to take a more active roll in the operation.

"They sent us up here to keep us out from under foot. Well, that is some bull shit right there, as Brig would say. We are going to strafe the damned planet until we find our missing friend. IS THAT CLEAR?" Milo said loudly.

"YES SIR!" the crew answered.

Sawyer's Revenge dropped into the upper atmosphere and Milo took his captain's shuttle and dropped away from the main ship. The shuttle was the name; that the Kyl navy gave it. That was a poor name for this vessel. It was called Brig's Fist by the ships crew, because it was not a shuttle at all, it was a miniature war ship, with the best guns and shield in the fleet. In fact the only ship that could stand toe to toe with it was the Revenge herself; and since they were both Milo's to command, that was not going to happen.

"Lt. Pepper you have the Revenge." Milo said over the com.

"Yes sir, I will keep her safe." Pepper said.

"See that you do Pepper." Milo said.

Milo smiled as he left the Revenge to go planet side and find his friend. Pepper was his baby sister and she was in and out of the naval academy in two short years. The girl was a genius, not that Milo was going to say so to her. When they built the Sawyer's Revenge, Milo was open to crew the new ship with whom ever he chose. The first choice was the chief, Brig called him Scotty and for some reason and it stuck. Milo wanted a few tough crew members, but he told Jamis and the Grand Counsel he did not want any Guardians on his ship, unless they were passengers. Jamis chuckled at first but Milo had some of Brig's leather in his back side, so Jamis took the statement seriously and Milo got his way. The speaker said the words Milo wanted to hear.

"Milo you have complete control over the ship and her crew." Jamis said.

Milo was a hard young man these days. But he was sharp eyed and open minded. When Milo was told his sister would be the first person to graduate in only two years; about half the normal time, he went to the academy and had her assigned to the Revenge behind her back. Milo had a first officer in mind, from his old crew but he decided to hang it up, resign his commission and stay on Kyl with his three mates and four children.

The day the ship was finished and was being ready to launch was the day before his sister was to graduate, so Milo ordered the launch to be stopped for a day and a half so that his sister could be onboard for the launch of her first ship assignment. Pepper was not like other Kylr girls, she was very thin and wiry, much like Korin. Her class mates and friends never resented her progress, most went as far as helping her as much as they could. Pepper was loved by everyone, for her mind and loving way. Pepper was also the hand to hand academy champion in self defense. When Pepper was called forward to receive her officer's certificate from Jamis; the entire planet roared with pride at the best officer in a hundred years to be commissioned.

In a surprise move, Jamis called Milo forward to pin Pepper's officer crests on her formal uniform. The Kylr people did not wear much as a race, so the formal wear was for very rare occasions only. Milo came forward and the crowd roared for him as well. He was the youngest captain in history and already held to be among the best ever.

"Captain Milo of the new flag ship Sawyer's Revenge will be pinning the new 1ˢᵗ Lt Pepper." Jamis said.

"Congrads little sister, I am proud of you. Who makes first lousy right out of the gate?" Milo said.

The crowd was very merry for all the graduates but they were ecstatic over Pepper. Pepper was not a glory hound she took her achievements in stride and moved to the next goal and worked on that one.

Milo quieted the crowd and made a speech of his own.

"I am very pleased to be the captain of the new flag ship Sawyer's Revenge. I am equally proud that my baby sister has earned the respect and admiration of our people, by the force of her will and deeds. It is for those reasons I am even more proud to announce Pepper will be serving as first officer on the Revenge starting now. This decision was approved by the entire crew of our vessel. We will be educating Pepper in the finer arts of running a ship." Milo said.

The crowd went wild and cheered so loud that Milo could not hear Pepper or Jamis who were both trying to get his attention. Finally, Pepper tossed good form aside and tugged on Milo's sleeve. He looked at her. Her tiny pretty face was a mask of horror. Jamis beside her was deeply concerned. Milo smiled.

"There can be no gain without risk." Milo said softly.

Jamis and Pepper read Milo's lips as if they could hear his voice. Milo's eyes were wild like an animal, calculating. Jamis thought at that moment the touch of Brigand sawyer and Jillian Robins on his race was indeed profound, and it a good thing for the Kylr to grow as a people if they were to continue into the future. The arrogance of the Kylr was almost gone; in its place was a new zest for the unknown and the untested. Here was Pepper, one moment cadet, the next moment the XO on the most powerful ship in the universe.

The very next day the brother and sister command team took the mighty Sawyer's Revenge out for her maiden voyage. The ship was a dream and Pepper was an excellent officer. She had the mix of pixie and hellcat down to a science. Her orders were never questioned or lightly given. Milo made a good choice in his choices for a crew, from Scottie to Pepper.

As the Fist dropped down to forty feet off the Grot plains Milo was running over all the things that brought him to Grot, gave him the command of the mighty Revenge and put his baby sister in his keeping. Life is strange.

A Bright blast off in the hills caught the pilot's eyes and he jumped in speed to get there before the area was abandoned. Milo was about to ask what he was doing, but he saw a second plasma blast and held his peace. The ship banked expertly and dove between the trees as Swoop made the mini war ship dance. The crew called this nut job, Swoop because when he flew, that is what he did. He might be a tad odd but he could thread a needle at light speed and in combat. He was by far the best stick man in the galaxy. In an air to air battle if you face Swoop, then you died. He was that good. His crazy flying style bothered everyone but Pepper, Milo and Scotty, who all knew him to be a fine officer and the most dedicated pilot in the known universe. Swoop would not even scratch his ship; if you shot at his ship he took it personally and went after you.

"There is a fracas down their skipper, if I did not know better; I would say that it is Lady Jillian down there in that mess." Swoop said.

"Oh man, it probably is her and Korin as well. Hey Swoops; are we in stealth mode?" Milo asked.

"Always sir." Swoop answered.

"Good. We need to watch and assist only if we have too. Korin is not the type to brook any interference in her fights, neither for that matter is Jillian these days. Wait, who the hell is that?" Milo asked.

Although; they did not know it at the time, Milo was about to meet the best friend and lover; who would be with him for the rest of his life. Tigra flashed through the trees and fired on Korin and then on Jillian. Swoop was impressed by the alien's crazy speed and precision.

"Damn it, that girl is a Karna hunter, she may get Jillian if this goes on much longer." Milo said tensely.

"I would not bet the farm on that one Milo. Jillian can take most Guardians with the Glave thing in her tiny hands, and she looks peeved to me." Swoop offered.

Milo was not happy about the pinched battle that he was forced to stay out of for safety reasons. Moreover, the Karna did not make war unless they were provoked, and Korin is the provocation type.

"Swoop takes us out of here, we are looking for Brig's body, up right or laid low, we have to find my friend." Milo ordered.

Swoop slowly pulled away so that the people on the ground would not know they were ever there. Milo was grim.

(ON THE FAR SIDE OF THE HILLS)

On the second day of his trek, Matho made the low foot hills. He did not know why he came here; he just knew that he was pulled by a feeling in his heart that this was the right direction. Matho had seen a few giant birds flying around looking for small game to eat; and they stayed away from the Pirz assassin wisely. There was also a three legged giant elephant like creature know to the Grot as the Domn. These creatures had the best poop for growing plants anywhere in the galaxy. They were said to be a solitary creature, but it was also said when the invincible Domn gather together life on Grot always changes. The Grot learned long ago not to hunt these creatures; The Domn can take a shot from a blaster at point blank range and suffer almost no damage at all. Their short trunk can pulverize stone into dust, and the weird three legged gate can become a blur fast run when they get spooked or mad. In either case, whatever is in front of them gets trampled flat. They are near fifty thousand pounds and their backs are thirty feet high. Matho actually walk beside one and it touched his shoulder with its giant trunk playfully. Matho scratched its shoulder and it rumbled happily. When Matho start to go up him into the hills the Domn stopped and crooned a deep goodbye noise and hung a right and wandered back into the open plains; that stretched for hundreds of miles. The plains were only broken by hills and the trees that grew around them.

"You better be this way Brig or I am going to be awfully put out" Matho said as he sat on a rock to rest.

Little did Matho know his friend was on the other side of this mountain? Matho drank some water and reflected on how beautiful Grot was; and how it was so unlike the race that shared the name. They were big, aggressive and ugly, where the planet was breathtaking and peaceful.

(BANG. . .Bang)

There was an echo of something that sounded like a pulse rifle. Matho put his canteen up and shifted into the rocks to a protected spot, incase he was the target out here today. He was not. Matho was on his guard now though and re-motivated to find Brig and finish this business so he could go home to the only girl he ever loved or ever would love; Marge.

Matho was not one to let his mind wander; and he had been in the middle of a civil war as a teenager, which he still was. Marge made him feel like the man he wanted to be, but she could get him killed if he thought about her instead of paying close attention to his mission.

The wind kicked up and Matho was sure he could smell the tell-tell sign that a space craft was near by or had recently been. He scanned the skies with his rifle cradled in his arm. He did not see a thing.

Milo flew over Matho and did not see him in the rocks as they went. Being invisible made it easy to move around on Grot without permission, but Milo would have acted in the same manner regardless of orders. Swoop banked the Fist and they were over one of the Grot oceans in the next instant. Milo was not happy about leaving Jillian to deal with a Karna, they were always a dangerous opponent; however, Milo was on a mission and that was more important. Brig was his friend but he must be found so that no other race could use his power for evil or personal gain.

"Check the monster fish on this marble Milo." Swoop said in his upbeat way.

Milo saw some amazing fish creatures jumping in and out of the water. There were birds and fish playing a game, the little fish would get eaten by the birds, and the bird were eaten by bigger fish that could jump thirty feet above the water. It was fascinating to watch. Again this is not why they were here so Swoop moved on.

"Hey skipper, Brig is an amazing guy, but he does not walk on or live in water, so he is not going to be out here." Swoop said.

Milo rubbed his face but he knew that Swoop was right. Brig was not out here.

"Turn this bucket around and let's search the plains and the foot hills again, only slower this time Swoop." Milo ordered.

"You got it skipper." Swoop crooned in his mad way.

The ship took a hard left and skimmed the water, dozens of huge water creatures tried to eat it, though it was unseen. Swoop believed that they had a build in radar of sorts and hunted by movement or sound. Swoop laughed and picked up the pace to avoid hitting or getting swallowed by a big water monster.

(OUT ON THE PLAINS)

Tarc saw the blur in the air as it went over his head and he turned and looked at it. Milo was watching and saw that the huge bovine was watching them; even though they were invisible.

"Swoop land this bucket, I have a hunch I want to check out." Milo said.

Swoop landed the Fist about sixty yards from the Tarocs and Milo walked out of the invisible ship and across the field to Tarc.

"Hello Kylr citizen." Tarc said.

The Tarocs made a slight bow of its massive four horned head. Milo smiled, his hunch was correct.

"Greetings sir; I believe you saw us fly over your head. I witnessed your ability to reason that we were there despite the fact you could see us, and made up my mind to ask you a question." Milo answered.

"What would you ask me?" Tarc asked.

"Where is Brigand Sawyer, our lost brother?"

CHAPTER 13: LET 'R RIP

Tiny was running as fast as he could, there were three or four followers that would not stop tracking him. They shot at him once. He was sure he was toast but he got out of the way and ran for it. Tiny could fight up close, but these attackers had distance weapons and they were pretty good with them.

"Jesus, what did I do?" Tiny said, as sweat ran down his face and body.

The attacker that looked like him; carried a wild weapon that could change size; Tiny knew this because; when they first spotted him watching the Karna from above; Tiny tossed a rock at her and the damn weapon became huge and deflected the stone. Worse the blue girl was one of those damn Guardian people, life sucked sometimes.

Korin was no longer on Oru's back; she was running without breaking stride for any reason. Oru rammed a path through anything he could not jump over and the girl followed him. Jillian saw Brig first and foolishly flashed the rocks by his head to get his attention. He hurled a rock at her; and then ran like a mad animal away. He did not know any of them. Korin saw that he did not know them and began to cry, secondly, she attacked him without mercy. Jillian bitch slapped her on her back and put the Glave to her throat and said only one word.

"NO!"

Korin decide to pick her fights, and Jillian was already crying.

"Okay, first we catch him and then we both decide if he still has a soul. I will not harm him until then Jillian, but if he is gone, we must take care of him, it is our responsibility to him as well as the universe." Korin said.

Jillian cried and put her head on Korin's shoulder, the lithe blue goddess held Jillian firmly in her arms.

"Don't cry Jillian, I love you and if there is anyway possible; we will save Brig and run away together. If not then I will never leave your side again, that way we can carry the burden together." Korin said.

"Oru stay with Jilly too, no leeve." Oru grunted in pain.

Jillian wiped her tears away and took a deep breath and smiled for her cherished ones. She turned and ran in the general direction Brig went. Korin and Oru ripped after her as the agile human girl cut a swift path into the forest.

"My God what a change Jillian has made." Korin said to herself with a deep affection in her heart for the girl.

Tigra saw the exchange between Brig and the trio and was confused. Tigra still had not realized that her alien friend was Brigand Sawyer. When your heart is on fire with desire, you head tends to not see the blatantly obvious. Tigra was confused but still professional, she decided to double her efforts to catch up and question the alien about the meaning of all this. Tigra had the advantage over Korin and Jillian because she had better natural senses and she could hear and smell the alien making a break for it.

In the end it did not matter how fast any of them were, Tiny was not going to get caught. Something deep inside of him broke open like a flower in spring and memories flooded back into his head of a time when he was a little boy covered in blood; his own. Two big boys were taking turns holding and beating him. They were both more than twice his size and three years his senior. A little girl of uncommon beauty came around the corner and screamed. The big boy who was doing the hitting turned and ran over and grabbed her. The girl was crying. The little boy saw her tears and his heart burst into flames. Suddenly, as if he had a wild wolf in his soul, the little boy snarl and yanked his left arm down and then snapped it up so violently the bigger boy caught it in his throat and began to cough up blood. The little boy grabbed a hand full of hair and kneed him in his nose shattering it.

"No don't hurt me, please!" The little girl screamed.

The little boy was on the back of the bigger boy biting his ear off and clawing his eyes out. The bigger boy tried to defend himself but not matter how hard he hit the little boy it no longer made any difference, the kid was changed, he was now a predator and the big boy was the prey. The thing that put the fear of God in the big boy was the little guy's eyes, they never blinked. The eyes were wild with madness and no mercy...none.

"Hey stop that, stop this instant!" yelled a police officer.

The cop ran up and was going to grab the smaller boy until he looked at him, and was repelled by the madness in the small child's eyes. The bigger boys were broken in many pieces and had to be taken to the Emergency room to keep them alive. The little girl told the police everything she saw, everything. The police officer would not allow anyone to touch the little boy, but decide to ask the small girl to coax the boy into the ER when blood starting running out of his mouth.

Later the police officer was told that nearly all of the little boy's ribs were broken and he had a punctured intestine and was bleeding to death. When the cop went to the boy's room, the girl was there and she told the boy, he could not die because he was her hero and heroes have to live so that the bad people would not hurt the weak like her. The boy did not speak he just smiled and squeezed the girls hand. The police officer was shocked when the families of the big boys were in the little boy's room. The mother of one of the big boys suddenly spoke.

"We are ashamed of our sons, they picked on you and nearly killed you, and they deserved what they got." The mom said in tears.

The little boy looked out the window and sighed; and then he spoke in a tiny hoarse voice.

"They had me beaten and I gave up any fight I had left in me...until they tried to hurt Jill. I...lost my temper. I am the one who should be ashamed." The little boy said and then his tiny face went hard as granite. "I will not allow Jill to be hurt by anyone, no matter the personal cost to me."

The change in the shy little boy was startling. When he began to talk about the girl's welfare he had a force of nature about him. The room was silent, until the girl Jill spoke.

"Silly brave boy, go to sleep, I will be here when you wake up." The girl said.

Everyone left the room except the girl she laid down and put her hands on the boys arm and her little face next to his and she sang softly. The boys face looked to gentle and serene as he fell off into a coma like sleep.

The police officer went to look at the boys who started the fight. They both looked like they had been attacked by a wild animal, they were so drugged up they did not know he was even there. The doctor came in and the cop stopped him.

"How are they?" The policeman asked.

The doctor actually laughed.

"If I did not see the boy who did this to them I would have thought I was on candid camera. That little boy, should have died from his injuries, I told him that. Do you know what he said?" The doc asked.

"What?" The cop said.

"He said he refused to die while Jillian was watching because it would break her tender heart. I have never seen such a strong will in anyone. That boy has the heart of a lion and just as much fight in him as well." The doc said.

"More like a wounded Wolf, once cornered it will kill anything to get free and will not die until his foe does." The cop said.

The doctor just nodded his head that he agreed and then moved on to his duties.

All of this sprang into Tiny's mind as he ran like an animal away from his foes. He stopped and noticed he had tears in his rust colored eyes. That little girl from his memory was special; he had loved her more than his own next breath and would kill or be killed protecting her. Tiny knew one thing now; he had to return and find that girl, his heart would not allow him to do less. Tiny was finished running as well. If they wanted to fight so damn bad, so be it, he was angry now and could feel the fire in his soul ignite. Tiny looked around and began to make plans to trap and destroy his pursuers.

(IN THE FIST)

"I can't believe he was right there and we missed him. Damn it if Korin jumps him; all might be lost. Stand on it Swoopy!" Milo snarled.

"Oh you know it baby." Swoop said.

The best pilot in the universe laughed like a giddy child as he made the Fist move so fast that he drop the cloak and went full out with everything the ship had. At the top speed only Pepper and Swoop could handle the Fist, it was traveling at near ten times the speed of sound without the jump drive. Swoop smoothly dropped the ship to the ground at the foot of the hills. It was right by where Matho entered the hills on foot, but Milo did not know that. Swoop stayed with the ship and made all the tech checks on his ship, to make sure it was always ready to rock. Milo ran out of the ship into the hills.

Tiny found a water source that spilled into a small lake. He jumped into the water and swam to the other side. He began to set up vine snares and tree branch traps that would knock the stuffing out of anyone who wandered into them. He was so busy that he did not notice Tigra sneaking up on him from above in the trees. Matho, however did see the Karna and it was about to jump on the man he was positive was Brigand Sawyer.

The Karna jumped from tree to tree and was close enough to pounce. Matho made a decision to distract the man and the beast at the same time and not give himself away yet. Matho picked up a stone and tossed it into the brush near Brig. Brig was on his feet and he had some wicked looking blades in his hands. The Karna hid in the trees and was silent, but it was done; Brig was alert and the Karna was foiled. Matho moved very slowly up and around them both. Matho never took his eyes off of either of them as he moved, neither was aware of him. That was very odd.

(COME TOWARD THE LAKE)

Oru had both girls on his mighty back again and he was
running at an incredible clip. When the lake popped up on his
right side, the Wira slowed and went toward it to drink. The girls
jumped down and drank and washed the dust out of their mouths.
Oru's eyes were on the far bank. He did not move but his eyes did
and Korin noticed.

"What is it Oru?" Korin whispered.

"We are being watched and Breeg was here not long ago. He is
still here Oru theenks." Oru said softly.

Jillian who was watching the trees saw Tigra for an instant
and then she pulled her Glave and dove into the water and swam
across the lake. Oru grabbed Korin like a sack of spuds and
leaped nearly all the way across the lake in one bound. Jillian
still beat them out of the water, and she was livid. Jillian
snapped the Glave to life and cut a tree in half. It was the one
Tigra was hiding in. The battle started at the moment.

Matho saw the whole thing and was unable to do anything to
stop it this time. Brig however, was now in plain sight and
watching the scene as well.

"You have sealed your fate pale woman." Tigra snarled.

"Don't sing it, baby, bring it." Jillian answered.

Tigra foolishly thought she could go blade to blade with Jillian.
They clashed and Tigra's dagger was shattered and Tigra's right
leg was lacerated as she retreated a step. The Karna was not a
coward; but she was also not a fool, she could see that the Glave

was going to make close combat impossible if she wanted to live. Tigra pulled out a small palm knife and threw it at Jillian.

"Bitch please." Jillian said as she reached up and caught it with her hand.

That was the opening Tigra hoped for, she shot Jillian with her blaster. Jillian stepped back stunned at the sight of blood running down her breast bone. Tigra smiled. Jillian looked at her and smiled back. All Tigra heard was the ribs on her left side snapping. She looked down and the Glave blade was inside her body. Jillian had extended a long thin blade out when she caught the knife, she made the opening to make the faster Karna hold still long enough to injure her.

"Pale girl, I salute you, well played." Tigra said.

"Shall we continue?" Jillian asked.

"Lets. If you could kindly remove your blade from my ribs I mean?" Tigra said.

Jillian pulled the Glave out of Tigra's ribs from the fifteen feet away where she stood. Jillian rubbed some yellow goop on her injury and cracked her neck. The Glave blazed and Jillian waited for Tigra to signal her readiness, then it was on.

Matho watched in awe of the two women, he had never seen such deadly grace and speed at the same time. The sheer force of their attacks rocked the trees. Matho tore his gaze away to see Brig watching still in confusion.

Jillian was slower but her strikes were far more powerful than the Karna's were. Tigra left a bouncing Betty in Jillian's path. Jillian did not see her do it and stepped on the mine. It blew up and knocked Jillian into a tree. The Glave energy kept Jillian from any serious damage but the wind was knocked out of her. Tigra was standing over Jillian in that instant and was going the shoot her in the face when a bolt of green energy slammed into her and sent her sprawling. Matho knew Brig was no longer watching as her friends voice roared through the trees.

"COWARD, ASSASSINS, BASTARDS, BACK JUMPERS!" Brig screamed and he charged.

Oru saw him coming and understood that Brig was not coming in friendship, so Oru attacked Brig to save the girls. Oru reached out for Brig to stop his forward movement and talk to him. Brig rolling blocked the huge arm and ducked under it and slashed Oru's belly with a short sword. Brig hit Oru in the head with the pommel of the sword when Oru dropped his head in pain.

"STOP!" Korin screamed as green energy slammed Brig into a tree.

That was a monster mistake. The rags of leather and hides that Brig had wrapped around his arms and his G-jen were burned away. Worse, the G-jen roared to life to protected Brig from Korin's energy. Brig still not knowing Korin, Jillian or himself burst into a corona of crimson energy. Oru jumped on Brig to try to stop him from killing his own true loves. Brig misunderstood Oru's gesture and hit him with a mega power seething right cross to the jaw. The bones in Oru's neck broke.

"Oh Shit!" Korin said frightened.

Jillian jumped up and went to see to Tigra. The Karna was down but alive. Jillian lifted her and carried her away to safety. Tigra woke up and saw that she was being carried by Jillian and she stiffened.

"Peace girl, I am not your enemy, it was all a mistake. We are trying to stop my lost lover from destroying the universe." Jillian explained.

Jillian put Tigra down behind some sturdy rocks and pulled out her vial of yellow goop and rubbed some on Tigra's lacerated leg. It began to heal at once. Tigra was confused, but a huge explosion forestalled any questions. The Guardians were fighting.

Matho watched Brig fight Korin, the girl he loved with the ferocity of a crazed beast. Matho decided that Brig was lost and he had to be killed. Matho loaded the special shells that Jamis made to kill Brig and he began to cry unwanted tears. Brig was the one person Matho looked up to and aspired to be. Matho put Brig in his sights but could not get a clear shot because of the trees. Matho got up and moved to a better spot. Tigra saw him and the rifle as he moved. She grabbed Jillian and yanked her around. Jillian saw him too and knew why he was there. Tigra's rifle was back where she was injured and the Glave in not a distance weapon.

"Korin help." Jillian screamed.

The noise from the battle was immense, so Korin did not hear Jillian. Jillian handed Tigra her Glave.

"If I die this is yours, for my mistakes." Jillian said humbly in her kind hearted way.

Jillian ran like a deer through the forest trying to reach Brig and Korin before the assassin lined up Brig for the kill. She tripped only once and then she went even faster, recklessly through the forest and just as she heard the pop from the rifle Jillian rammed into Brig's back. The bullet went into Jillian's back and came out and lodged into Brig's shoulder. Brig jerked around ready to fight and his heart stopped.

"NO." Brig said as tears burst out of his eyes.

"Brig are you okay?" Jillian stood there wobbling as blood gusted out of her chest.

"Brig...yes that is my name. Oh my God!" Brig said.

Brig jumped forward and grabbed Jillian as she was about to fall. He held her in his arms and then ripped his cloak off and tossed it on the ground. Brig gently laid Jillian on it. He inspected her wound and then looked at his wrist in disgust.

"You better damn well help me this time you piece of shit!" Brig seethed.

Brigand Sawyer took the deepest breath of his life and placed both hands on his one true love. The crimson aura was all around them. Jillian's eyes were closing to death's grip, Brigand sent all of his power into her body. This is not a gift without cost. The flesh on his own back and arms began to be annihilated; Brig was trading his life for Jillian's. Jillian knew it and was too weak to stop him. Hell nothing could stop her man.

(BITCH SLAP).

Brig was knocked rolling by a hard right hand from the only other woman he had ever loved. He looked at Korin and his memory of her came back to him. Korin's eyes were gushing tears and she was mad as hell.

"Not this time hero, you are not dying today and neither is Jillian. We can help her together without killing us." Korin said holding out her hand to Brig.

Blankly, as if in a fog, Brig reached out and took her hand. They walked the few steps to Jillian and then held hands and made the most amazing swirl of colors you ever saw. Jillian closed her eyes but her chest rose and fell in perfect rhythm.

Meanwhile, Milo came over the hill and saw Matho fire his weapon. Milo also saw Jillian take a life ending shot in the back. Milo would have killed Matho, but the young man was crying like a child and mumbling, it was all a mistake. Milo ran down the hill and lost sight of Matho. Tigra was coming up the hill knife in hand, she pointed to the left of Milo and he turned to see Matho stumbling toward him. Milo hit the young man in the forehead with the butt of his rifle and grabbed Tigra's arm as she lunged at Matho with a knife. Milo is cock strong, and he held Tigra firmly in place.

"Sugar, there has been enough blood shed today, let's just carry him down to the others and see if we can help?" Milo said.

Tigra looked at Milo for the first time and the handsome captain smiled at her. Tigra was shocked her heart was pounding. So was his and she could here it. Together they hauled Matho and his gear down to where Jillian was being healed up. Brig looked up with a deep look of dread and Korin did as well.

"Matho? Wake that little shit up and ask him what he put into Jillian before I kill him." Korin said.

Tigra was going to whip Matho's ass good. He tried to kill her friend and ended up hitting a valiant warrior by mistake. Milo held her off.

"Let me handle this; Matho is Brig's pupil and he is very tough and resourceful." Milo said.

Milo sat Matho up against a tree and got a cup full of water from the lake and threw it in his face. Matho woke up surrounded by familiar faces.

"Hello guys, what happened?" Matho asked.

"Matho you tried to put one in me when my back was turned, not cool young man. You hit Jillian instead of me, what the hell was in that shell?" Brig asked.

"Oh Shit, is Jillian okay. Never mind, don't answer that; just listen. Jamis made those shells to kill Brig in case he was a soulless monster, but, I have the antidote in my bag, yellow tipped fluid filled darts, quickly." Matho said with angry tears in his hard eyes.

Korin rummaged through the bag and found them and was about to inject Jillian; when Milo stopped her dead. Korin was so mad she would have killed him if not for Brig; He touched Korin's shoulder spoke to Milo.

"What is it Milo?" Brig asked.

"I trust Matho, he is a straight shooting fighter. However, he did not pact those darts man, Jamis did, who knows what the hell is in them." Milo said.

"Are you questioning Jamis honor?" Korin snarled.

"He sent Matho to kill Brig." Milo said back with equal strength.

Korin recoiled as if punched in the face. Milo was right. Korin looked at the dart in her hand and shook, her lover was dying and she did not know what to do. Suddenly Brig yelled and startled everyone.

"ORU I NEED YA." Brig screamed.

"Breeg?" A hoarse voice said as a huge bulk came forward.

Oru was bleeding to death and only partially from the sword wound Brig gave him. The Wira was in the final moments of his life. Brig started to shake as he approached Oru. Brig put his hand on Oru tummy and made his hands glow. Oru instantly relaxed and sighed.

"There, I made the pain go away until I can heal you properly buddy. I need you to tell me what your super sniffer says is in this dart liquid?" Brig asked.

"Give Oru the dart, I weel smell'em." Oru groaned.

Korin handed the dart to Oru and he sniffed it and then he said a word Brig did not know.

"Sarn." Oru said.

Korin lunged forward and grabbed the dart and ran to Jillian and sank the dart tip all the way to the hub in Jillian's heart. She never moved after she took the empty dart out and tossed it a side. Korin began to glow Bright mist green, she placed her hands on Jillian and began to heal her once again.

"Sorry about the knife wound Oru, I forgot who I was. Here let me fix that." Brig said.

"No, let Oru die; knifey wound not kill Oru. Oru die from own choice to help Brig." Oru said as he slumped and his eyes closed.

Brig could feel Oru's heart slowing to a stop.

"NO, not you, you cannot die, I will not let you die for me." Brig started to glow like a red neutron star.

Four darts flew by Brig's head and into Oru. Brig turned his

head eyes glowing. Matho was behind him with two more
darts, in his hands.

"Go on heal him Brig; the yellow juice is a super cure." Matho
said.

   Matho walked over to Milo and handed him a dart, and then
looked at Tigra. The Karna was totally engrossed with Milo and
did not see Matho approach them. Milo smiled and he held up the
dart.

"Healing,... good times and a pretty girl." Milo said.

   All Tigra heard was pretty girl, and she barely even looked
down when he sank in the dart and let the fluid healing from
within.

"You think you might want to spend some time with a blue guy?
Karna don't usually mate or even couple with non-Karna;
however, I fancy you." Milo said.

"I think I am ready for a man in my life and you are about as fine
a man as I could hope for." Tigra said.

   It was hours, even with the yellow healing fluid before Jillian
could sit up and talk. Oru was still down for the count and Brig
had his eyes closed and was concentrating on the healing the
entire time. Oru was so close to death that Korin was afraid that
the bonding link between Brig and Oru might kill Brig as well if
Oru died. Brig was a natural born hero, and he was determined
not to loose his friend, no matter the cost to himself.

   Matho and Tigra made peace. Milo and the two of them set up
a good camp and set a guard to watch for any Grim'oc or the type
that jumped you in the dark. The camp was warm and the big
hunter killers did not go to the hills, it was not an area with lots

of game.

Tigra cuddled up to Milo and they went to sleep holding each other. Korin cradled Jillian in her arms; and the Guardian was still glowing with energy as she continued to heal Jillian's injuries and the poison in her blood. Jillian watched Brig when she was strong enough to keep her eyes open. She felt like she was dying, because he was so close and she could not touch or help him. Once again; Brig was alone to do what must be done.

CHAPTER 14: JAR'S PLAN

In the capitol city the former leader of the Kyl Guardians sat with Elor the 3rd, king of all the Grot. Jar was a bitter ass these days. He was once the most powerful man in the galaxy and now he was not even respected. The only person that seemed to give him the proper due, was the king of the beastly war like Grot. They talked and played a game very similar to Earth chess most every day.

"You are not here with me this day Jar. I think your mind is out there looking for the body of the hero." Elor said.

"Hero, hardly; Brigand Sawyer was a hot headed youth with more guts than brains." Jar rasped.

"Perhaps, but it was you who made him a Guardian, was it not?" Elor asked.

Jar got up and walked over to look out the palace window. He thought on the question for a long while unmoving. To Elor it seemed that the Kylr was trying to decide something. Jar came to a decision and turned to address the king.

"I was sent to Brig's planet on a mission from Jamis himself. He gave me the G-jen I placed on Brig's arm. He told me I would know the who and the when to place it. Well, I guess he was right. Brigand Sawyer has done nothing to wrong me, but because of him, my status among my people has changed. I do not want to be in my current position for all of eternity." Jar said.

The king looked at him; he took no offense at Jar's last comment, because it had nothing to do with the Grot. Jar simply wanted to regain his passed glories; like every man did. Jar was nearly immortal so he could regain those glories, where most men grow old and die sullen and alone with regrets.

"No doubt you have a plan?" Elor inquired.

"No doubt indeed. If Brigand Sawyer gets himself killed out there, then Korin and Jillian will be heart sick and they will likely disappear into the universe some where unknown to live out their lives. If Brig comes back, Korin will give up command of the Guardians and I will be needed again. Either way I win." Jar explained.

"I always wondered if the Guardians were capable of selfish acts or out right treason against the state. You have just displayed both of those things. I find you to be the right kind of friend the crown of Grot needs to have." Elor said.

"I was wondering if it would be possible to have the area Brig is in to be bombed or shelled from space." Jar asked.

Elor looked at him and smiled. Here was a bad man who would cheat and kill to get what he wanted. Elor loved to butcher things; he was by nature a mean bastard most of the time. He was only calm and reserved when his powerful son was around. Elon was his Achilles heel, he could not beat him and he could not kill him either, unless in open combat. Elon was a problem.

"I do have a few contacts with pirates that would be glad to help us out for some gems or gold. Is your plan worthy of funding it personally, or not really?" Elor asked slyly.

"I am quite rich actually, and have no issue with paying pirate to take care of my little problem." Jar answered.

The plans were made and the pirate lord Slag was contacted to rid Grot of a Guardian or two. Jar did not want to kill the lovely Jillian because he still wanted to have a child with her, but he hated Korin and wanted her dead more than he wanted Brigand Sawyer to never come back. If Kerra found out she would find a way to kill Jar. Kerra was a busy woman; it was highly unlikely she would ever know anything happened until much after the fact.

Slag and his partner Kor came in a royal Grot transport, privately in the dead of night. If Elon saw either one of these trash, he would have killed them. Elor could not let that happen. Elor loved this cloak and dagger stuff. Jar thought he was using Elor, but the king wanted to help him. Secretly Elor wanted to kill all the Guardians and take over the galaxy, just like old times.

"Greetings Slag." Elor said.

"Cut the shit Grot, what do you want done or who do you want killed?" Slag said.

Jar realized that Slag and Elor had done business before and he was betting that Elor gypped them in the past by Slag's attitude. Jar's belief proved right the next moment.

"No matter what the job is, you pay in full up front; or no deal." Slag graveled out.

"Fine by me but I am not the client, he is." Elor pointed in the shadows.

When Jar walked into the light both pirate reached for their weapons, Jar ignored the stupidity. Pirate weapons could not harm a Guardian. Jar sat down and gestured for the pirates to joint him. They did, more out of curiosity than fear.

"I want people killed and the area to be bombed hard. NO survivors; or I know two pirates that will be dead. If you betray me your dead, if you mess up the job your dead, if you get caught your dead. I will do the honors myself. Do you want the job?" Jar asked.

The two pirate scum looked at Jar and were profoundly confused by his odd actions. Were not the Guardians supposed to stop people like them from doing the very thing he just asked them to perform? They were also intrigued by the whole thing to be honest. Slag stepped forward and looked Jar in the eye with all three of his; he stood there studying the Guardian for a while. Finally he seemed satisfied and turned to the Karna.

"What say you partner?" Slag asked.

"I want to know what the gain is, before we discuss the risk." Kor said looking at Elor.

The giant Grot plopped down in his chair looking decidedly mirthful about the meeting all in all. Kor was a happy evil man-cat and he liked the king. They had a scum bag connection if you will; they understood each other pretty much and that made them easy business partners. No big surprises.

"I would like to hear Jar's offer as well, I am only facilitating this job, not contracting it." Elor explained.

All eyes turned to Jar. The blue man rubbed his chin meaningfully and sat on the chair next to the king's own seat.

"I will give you...his weight in gold and gems; IF, you complete the job." Jar said pointing at the Chrisalian pirate, who was a big man, heavy as well.

Kor looked at Slag and smiled. A payment that weighed what his heavy friend did; was a fine payout indeed. Kor was ready to iron out the risk details at this point being satisfied the risk would be worth the reward. This Guardian might lie about the reward but the king would not allow a deal to go south. Elor had a great deal of dirty work done by the Chrisalian pirates and would not let his business be interrupted by Jar.

"What is the plan Jar?" Kor asked.

"Sooner or later Brig will be found. When they use the com to report in; you zero in on where that is and bomb the region to ashes. My friend the King will make sure any Grot patrols are rerouted elsewhere for safety. Nobody wants Elon on their backs, so caution is a must. Once the Job is complete, flee the galaxy to a predetermined spot, your payment will be delivered there on confirmation of kills." Jar explained.

"Sounds like a sound plan Jar. You are a pirate at heart mate." Slag said in his gruff voice.

The thought made Jar smile; perhaps he really was just a little bit evil down deep. Hell Korin could have told him that. Korin came to Jar's mind, she must be killed or Jar's plans worthless.

"Does your ship have stealth capability? If not then you better stay behind the moon until you are needed. If you can stay close so you can hit and run." Jar said.

"We are pirates man, we have the best stealth gear in the universe; it is part of the required job credentials." Kor explained.

"Good, you two better get off planet until you are to perform your task. Here take this as a token of my commitment to the job." Jar said as he tossed a gem to Kor.

The Karna pirate caught the stone and his eyes went wide. It was a Romeal ruby of perfect quality. The gem alone would be payment enough for the job. Kor was confused, and why would anyone give up a gem of this quality and rare as they come. Jar must have understood the look because he answered Kor's thoughts.

"I want them dead at all costs." Jar said.

Slag and Kor bowed slightly and walked into the dark with the Grot guards that brought them to the palace. They were taken back to their ship. Once on board Kor cautioned his long time partner.

"We had better not fail or that Guardian will hunt us down and butcher us like beasts. I sense madness in him, jealousy and envy. We better have a back up plan in case this falls apart. Say, like fingering Jar for the whole thing." Kor said.

"Hey, Jar said if we point him out he will kill us!" Slag added.

"He would if he could. We will put the other Guardians on his back; therefore he will not be able to deal with us, because they will deal with him.

"Good plan Kor." Slag admitted.

Kor was the thinker in this partnership and Slag was the muscle and the evil. They got rich together because they could handle anything and anyone; one way or another. These two left a wake of bodies and death where ever they went. They had no mercy and no remorse; that is what made them the best. They trusted only each other and no one else, that fact kept them alive.

(ELSEWHERE IN THE PALACE)

Rok was not happy when he heard that Jamis expected Matho to Kill Brig and Brig would finish off the boy, therefore all the loose ends would be tied up. Rok told the Speaker he was ashamed that he ever looked up to him. More, the giant told Jamis that he needed a reality check and an attitude adjustment if he wanted to continue to lead the Kylr. To that revelation Jamis decide to give some thought. Rok was very popular and more and more Kylr mirrored his point of view. It was all of-course Brigand Sawyer's influence that brought it all on. The Kylr were once more a proud active race. They lost their arrogance and got back to what made them great; hard work.

"When Brig gets back, and he is restored to health, life in the galaxy is going to be different. The old ways have pressed our race to near extinction; a new era is upon us." Rok said.

Elon was impressed by his friend's commitment to his friend and the future of his people. Elon believed that Rok would make a very fine speaker of Kyl; he was a man of morals and vision, at least since Brig came to roost.

"We can only hope for the safe return of our friend if he is still our friend. I too think that sending Matho to possibly try to kill Brig; is a poor idea. If he should miss, it could set a tragedy in motion." Bello said.

"Yes it could; however I gave Matho special ammunition to kill even Brig." Jamis said.

"YOU DID WHAT!" Rok roared.

"Would you let a mad man run free in the universe causing millions of deaths and destroying entire planets? I cannot allow that to happen. We are the Kylr, and we keep the universe safe. Brigand Sawyer is our problem and one way or another he has to be dealt with here and now." Jamis said sternly.

"You better hope old man that is works out the right way. If so much as a hair on Jillian's or Korin's lovely heads is harmed, it is you who I will hold responsible. More, your place of respect will be tainted and I will see you removed old man." Rok said.

Jamis had never seen the huge Guardian furious before. Rok was a calm thoughtful man; because of his greater size and power, Rok made sure he gave the impression of calm and security to all of the people around him. Now, he was angry and belligerent. He read Jamis the law in front of God and everyone.

"Perhaps, I have acted rashly, but I did so for the greater good, you have to at times make the greatest sacrifice for the many." Jamis said thoughtfully.

(IN THE FOREST BY THE LAKE)

Milo woke up with Tigra tucked into his side purring softly, it was very nice. Milo was a solitary man, but he no longer wanted to be. Matho was cooking something for Korin and Jillian, he was very handy during outings from what Bello and Rok told him after the rebellion on Pirz was over. Brig was still working hard to save Oru. The Wira did not look any better.

"Good morning Milo." said a voice in his ear.

Tigra sat up and smiled and then cat stretched her body. Her lovely powerfully built lean body made Milo's heart jump. She felt the same about him. She looked at Brig though with a sad look, so Milo asked the obvious question.

"Did something happen between you and Brigand?" Milo asked.

"Yes, he captured me one night, when he still did not know himself. He told me I reminded him of a girl he used to know, but could no recall her name. He showed me what letting someone close to you can mean to your soul. I will always want to be his friend, but I don't love him. I know that now...that I met you Milo." Tigra said with a smile.

Milo grabbed her in his powerful hands and held her close to him. They embraced and love was born between them.

"Break it up and come eat or go hungry." Matho said jokingly.

Korin and Matho had made their peace over Jillian's injury. Jillian looked nearly well, just a bit of peeky was left in her sweat face. The glow of deep love was back on Jillian's face and it looked very good there. Korin wore the perpetual smile she used to have before Brig was thought to be dead. Only Oru was cause for sadness, the Wira seemed to be dying.

There was a sound over head as a mini hurricane moved the water of the lake around. All the faces were shocked and battle ready except for Milo who was silently shaking with mirth. Finally the Kylr captain could not hold it any more and started rolling with laughter.

"We are not under attack; it is only the Fist landing on the lake." Milo said.

At that moment the lake was still and the ship became visible. Before them in the water was the most beautiful ship any of them had ever seen. It opened up and a happy looking joker came out and ripped off his shirt and pants and dove into the cool water and swam to them in his drawers.

154   GUARDIANS: LOST ON GROT

"Did you call for a ride skipper?" Swoop asked.

Milo had to smile at his mad hatter of a pilot. The others seemed equally amused by the man. Swoop stood up and looked at all the people in the camp. A green tinted Pirz assassin, a Karna hunter who was holding hands with his skipper, the lovely and volatile Korin, and the Amazon queen of the sky Lady Jillian of the Glave and Brigand Sawyer himself stand next to the craziest looking creature Swoop had ever seen.

"Did you call in our good news to Jamis in the capital Swoopy?" Milo asked.

"I called it in skipper, but it was Jar that took the message." Swoop said and made a face.

"Pilot, what is the matter, why did you make that face. It troubles me for some reason I cannot say." Korin asked.

Swoop looked at Milo for help to explain, well to explain Swoop, so that they would understand what he was going to say. In the end he just let'r rip.

"That guy seemed to damn happy to hear we found Brig and he was okay, himself anyway. He did not ask who I was or who found Brig, he just wanted to chat about where we were and then he made small talk, it was odd." Swoop said.

Korin was next to Brig looking startled. Milo looked at them and had an epiphany. He grabbed Matho by the arm and ran to Jillian towing Tigra with the other hand.

"Get Jillian and your gear into the Fist now, Swoop get the Fist shields up!" Milo yelled.

Swoop hit the water like a dolphin and was in the ship with the shields up in less than ten seconds. Matho and Milo brought Jillian to the ship, Tigra pulled along the gear. Swoop dropped the shield long enough to literally yank the people and the gear into the ship. Jillian sat weakly by the hatch and screamed at Korin and Brig to get on the ship.

"NO!" Brig shouted.

"We cannot leave Oru and he is too big to enter the ship." Korin said.

"OH SHIT." Swoop said, "We are so out of time kids!"

The Pilot snapped the hatch shut and punched it, as the warheads rammed into the forest where they had just been. The entire forest was a fire ball inferno.

"BRIG...KORIN...Oru!" Jillian cried.

CHAPTER 15: PAYBACK

The explosion registered on the planetary defense system. Elon was in the war room thirty second after the klaxon went off to alert the population there was a threat in the atmosphere. Rok was next to Elon when the prince arrived.

"What do you have commander, are we under attack?" Elon asked.

"There was a major explosion south-east of the capitol about seventy nine miles away. The forest range out there is burning with chemical fire, there is no base or patrols in the area; on the ground or in orbit my prince." The commander answered.

"None, we have none in that area. That is not possible. Look into it commander; I want to know why we are uncovered and who is responsible." Elon roared.

Rok looked out the wall sized windows at the plains and touched his wrist com.

"Bello, we need to talk." Rok said calmly into the device.

(IN THE PIRATE SHIP)

Kor was checking the sensors to see if there were any life-signs in the forest that was being shelled from their own ship. They were in stealth mode, however when firing they came slightly visible with every burst of their canons, or in this case missiles.

"Cease fire Slag, well done partner. I don't see any signs of life down there, we just got rich." Kor said.

"Yeah, but if we don't get moving we are not going to be spending any of it." Slag retorted.

What the Pirates did not know was, at that moment Swoop was coming in hot and he was mad as hell. Once again Swoop was a tad off his rocker and you don't shoot at his ship unless you want to die, and they blew up his people as well. Swoop was unhinged. Milo had everyone strap in.

"Make sure they don't get away Swoopy." Milo said.

"Don't insult me skipper, they never had a chance, the moment they fire on my ship." Swoop seethed.

Tigra was terrified she had never been in the craft this fast and with a pilot as completely nuts at the helm, she was not sure she ever would be again. Jillian on the other hand was heart sick, but alert. Jillian sat in the navigators chair right behind the pilot. She leaned forward and squeezed Swoop's shoulder.

"Get them Swoop!" Jillian hissed in his ear.

"Yes, ma'am." Swoop said.

Brig's Fist was in the atmosphere and picking up speed. Jillian watched the scope for the other ship or ships, but Swoop just watched the view screen, he was in his element. God save anyone he opposed. The other ship fired their last salvo just as Swoop banked away from them. Swoop smiled and barrel rolled the ship back on itself. The pirates did not see the Fist because it was in stealth mode as well. Swoop knew where they were now; at this point there was no escape.

The entire pirate ship rocked from the sudden impact. Their shield protected them from the blasts but it still shook the ship hard.

"What hit us Slag?" Kor asked.

Slag was on the scope looking and there was nothing there. He tried heat, exhaust, ion trials and came up with squat. There was nothing out there. The ship rocked hard again. Kor jump over the instrument panel and landed next to Slag; he also did not see anything.

"We are in trouble Kor. There is another ship out there in stealth mode and it is fast enough that I can't get a lock on them and neither came the Nav computer; so we can get a shot off at them." Slag said.

"Are the shields going to be able to protect us? If so I say we run for it." Kor said.

Slag did not answer, he just hit the star drive controls and the ship jumped to light speed instantly. Slag smiled and patted his partner on the back. They had an uneasy laugh. Both of them knew how close they came to being destroyed.

"Jar better pay off or he is going to pay another way after this." Kor said.

The Chrisalian pirate was going to answer but the ship rocked and then moaned and dropped out of light speed into drift mode.

"What..."Kor asked.

The ship bucked hard again and then again from another direction.

"Oh God, they knocked out the star drive and there is more than one ship out there after us." Slag said.

Slag was wrong it was only Swoop living up to his name; he did not speak when he was working, his mind and the ship were one. The Fist danced, looped and banked at near light speed. No computer could make the calculations to fly like Swoop did, and none could find him to shot him down. Swoop was without a peer of any kind when piloting a craft. Swoop was only limited by the craft, and Swoop always knew what his ships could do or not do better than the engineers that designed and built them.

"Don't destroy them Swoop." Tigra said.

That stopped Swoop in mid loop, Swoop leveled out and stopped firing his canons. He turned and looked at Tigra with a question on his face.

"I want to catch them and make sure all the guilty are made to pay. If you shoot their asses off, they are not going to be able to talk Swoop." Tigra explained.

"OK." Swoop answered.

Milo tapped his com and spoke into it. The Revenge jumped out of light-speed just a thousand yards to the Fist's starboard side.

"Hey Swoop, couldn't get the job done without me?" Pepper teased.

Swoop smiled, he loved Pepper and everything about her, her voice was one of the best things about her; It made his heart glow when she said his name.

"No, I tore them a new one Pep, but our skipper's kitten wants to capture the trash; instead of putting it out. I need you to lock on that ship and hold them while I board it." Swoop said.

"What ship?' pepper asked.

Swoop nailed the pirate ship with ten hard plasma canon blasts making it visible. Swoop knock out the power source expertly. Milo and Pepper both snickered at the man's amazing skills. Swoop could have been a surgeon if he wanted to, but he loved to fly more.

"Oh yes, that ship." Pepper giggled.

The Revenge grabbed the pirate ship in a tractor lock and held it deathly still. The Fist blew the cargo hatch off and flew the hatch of the Fist right up to the hull and locked on. Milo grabbed his weapons and headed toward the hatch. Tigra slammed his butt back down in the seat. Beside Tigra was where Matho stood, rifle in his hands and his blades lining his forearms.

"We hunted Brig, and we fought your people foolishly, we have a debt to repay, and repay it we will; right here and right now...alone!" Tigra announced.

"Good luck." Jillian said.

The Pirz and the Karna went aboard the Pirate ship. The pirates saw them. Slag was going to jump out and attack, but Kor stopped him wide eyed.

"Oh Shit, we are so screwed. That is Tigra, she is one of my race and she is the best and Brightest of all my people." Kor said.

Slag looked at his fearless partner and wonder; what could make this butcher hold his ground?

"So we don't attack?" Slag asked.

"Hell yes we attack, but attack the green male to distract Tigra or we will be the dead ones." Kor said.

   The two pirates snuck up and around the two hunters so they could back jump them. Tigra was going to alert Matho that they were being set up, but she could see Matho's eyes tracking them already and so was the muzzle of his rifle. She smiled at him. That young man would make a damn fine partner on jobs.

"Okay, wait for them to pass by that crate of melons and then we kill the male." Kor said.

   Slag was not new at this and said nothing just nodded slightly. The pirates tensed to attack, but paused as something clicked by their feet.

(BOOM)

   The stun grenade went off and it sent the two frazzled pirates into the bulk-head behind them. They tried to get up as they saw Matho and Tigra coming toward them; however they could not. Tigra seemed amused and confused. Matho explained.

"The grenade is my own design; it shocks the nervous system as well as explodes. Therefore, they are not going to get up and fight, even though they want to desperately." Matho explained.

   Yes, this man would be a great partner on jobs. The Pirz assassin was smart and tough; he would never risk a friend unless he could not do the task alone. Tigra was impressed. Together they tied and bound the pirates and tossed them in the Revenge's Brig when Pepper sent a shuttle to pick up the Prisoners. The Fist slipped back inside the Sawyer's Revenge and

home. When Swoop and Milo were on the bridge of the
Revenge with their guests; Swoop asked Pepper to do him a
favor.

"Pepper darling, could you be so kind as to blow that ratty piece
of shit out of my beautiful skies?" Swoop said.

(GIGGLES)

"Why yes kind sir; it would be my pleasure." Pepper said.

Pepper was not the type of girl to let a great opportunity go by
unused. She opened up every single one of the forward gun ports
and hit the pirate ship with it all at once. The pirate vessel
disappeared in what looked like a star going nova. Not even tiny
bits of flotsam were left.

"Nice." Swoop said.

"Okay that was fun. Swoop, get this bucket moving, we have
some asses that need kicked on Grot." Milo said in a hot
tempered voice.

To say the Revenge was fast would be a woeful
understatement. There was no known craft that could match its
speed or agility, not even close; and with Swoop at the helm,
even a great vessel was no match for the pride of the Kyl fleet.

***(A great vessel is a Kylr Manowar: it was thought to be
perfect in everyway; until Sawyer's Revenge was built.)

(IN THE PALACE ON GROT)

Bello and Jamis were astounded at the speed and ferocity of

the Grot command. Elon took over the entire operation. Jamis believed that Elon thought that Brig and his friends were in the area that was bombed. Elon was afraid Brig had lost his mind but he wanted to make sure before having him hunted. Now however, if any of the Kylr were killed or if Matho was killed then the Pirz would be on the war path. Headaches, that is all that the prince had. He was so unhappy about the lot his in life that brought him to this place; he was determined to make the guilty pay.

"What is the word Elon, any updated news?" Rok asked.

"I am being told there was at the least two ships involved, and both got away. The area that was bombed; was hit with a hell-fire warhead and several smaller warheads that tore down the forest; the area is still burning with chemical fire uncontrollable. I will have a full report as soon as it comes available." Elon said.

"You seem to have things well in hand." Bello said with no sarcasm.

(ELSEWHERE IN THE PALACE)

"They did it, they actually did it and I can rest easy now that my plan is well under way. All we have to do is; quietly confirm Brig is dead, hopefully Korin is dead as well!" Jar said.

Elor looked at his silly companion and thought to himself "This one would not be fit to lead an entire people, he was much too petty of a person." Moreover; there was going to be fall out if a Guardian was killed on Grot soil. The deaths meant nothing to the king, but the trouble they would bring on his planet had to be managed. A brilliant idea just came to him. He would blame Elon, after all, was it not Elon who wanted a guardian buried on Grot and by doing so; Elon brought all of the other Guardians here as well. Yes, it was all Elon's fault, and that was the ticket.

"You seemed lost in thought for a moment Elor?" Jar inquired.

"Yes, I have decided to blame my son for the entire affair. The bombing, the Guardians being on Grot, the deaths of the Mercs and the Grot guards as well." The king said pleasantly.

"What if he decides to fight you on it, what then?" Jar asked.

It was common knowledge that Elon was by far the most powerful Grot warrior, the king though large was not Elon's match in combat, and no Grot was. For that matter neither was nearly anyone else in the galaxy except the Guardians.

"He will not sidestep the charges; he has too much pride and honor, two things I do not have to deal with personally; to let anyone else take the blame. Elon will embrace the blame and make reparations, you mark my words. However, the public opinion of my son will fall and he will not seek my throne for years afterwards." Elor said happily.

Oh how extremely wrong Elor was, and soon he would find out the cost of that error.

CHAPTER 16: ALIVE & DANGEROUS

In what was once the beautiful Grot forest; there were three figures standing against the onslaught of fire power. The man was a crimson sun; he had blood coming out of his mouth from gritting his teeth and clenching his jaw. The woman was nearly naked, she tossed up her shield while running a tad too slow to save her skin and garments. The green aura burst out of her and her muscular body was covered in a heavy sheen of sweat. This was not the amazing part. The third member opened their mouth and sang and the flames died down and away from the other two.

From high about the once forest; all that could be seen were flames and heat and possibly radiation. There was no way for the universe outside the hellish nightmare to know that three candles still burned in the winds of fate. Neither, could the three lives within the hell know that there were efforts being made to find them and ascertain if they were alive or dead. Alone and completely exhausted they carried on without the benefit of hope. All they had was blind stubborn determination not to die; so that whoever was responsible was paid back ten fold.

"Brig are you okay, you're bleeding a lot?" Korin asked.

"I'll live; but your blue butt is currently pink and raw doll face." Brig said.

Korin smiled at his ever present playfulness even in the face of complete disaster, like now for instance. Oru was the problem, the Wira were a mysterious lot, and Oru has broken a life rule among the Wira and it has basically killed him. When Brig thought the bomb had killed them all, at the eleventh and a half hour he tossed all his power into a blast that he sent straight up. It had the same effect as setting a back fire to burn against a forest fire; it cancelled out most of the damage around Brig and Oru. The real problem was Oru, the Wira was dying and Brig could not keep healing him and keep the inferno away. Brig was getting desperate; his friend was dying and it felt like he was as well. Oru took the choice out of Brig's hands. He opened his mouth and sang and what looked like and rainbow came out of his mouth. The fire around the trio flickered and went out.

"Oh shit, Oru don't do that!" Korin shouted.

The Wira paid her no mind at all, he sang on as if he heard nothing which was the truth. Oru was beyond hearing or seeing anymore, he decided his last act of life was to trade his life for Brig's. Oru made the choice when they came looking for Brig to sacrifice himself for his beloved bondling and friend. It is what Brig would do...had done not once but three times to Oru's knowledge. Oru was very proud of Brig and felt that he must be paid back and live for Jilly and Korin.

"What is happening, what is Oru doing?" Brig said in horror.

Oru was beginning to shrink. The Wira's large golden eyes were blinking slowly as if he were using the greatest concentration. Oru was dying rapidly. It is a total mystery how the Wira's powers and abilities work. However, it is common knowledge that the Wira are a match for even a Guardian. Therefore, the Wira were an extremely powerful elusive race; they shunned attention and did not mix with non-Wira...except for Oru, he loved Brig and Jillian and Korin more than he wanted to live.

Korin was hysterical and crying; she was completely unable to speak. She knew what Oru was doing and she was powerless to do anything but watch her friend wither away. Brig looked at Oru and he knew as well, but Brig refused to loose Oru.

Something inside of Brig broke. As his own angry tears began to fall, he gritted his teeth, set his feet and opened every once of energy in his body and then some; Brig pulled the energy out of the ground, and the air. Brig closed his eyes and whispered to Korin.

"Get down." Brig said.

When Brig said that short phrase in a soft voice it frightened Korin; she dropped to the ground and crawled toward Oru.

Brig opened his eyes and tears of blood ran down his face as he let loose a blast so powerful it shook the entire planet of Grot.

(ON THE REVENGE)

There was a brilliant flash that the crew of the Revenge could see even in hyperspace with the star drive growling as Swoop pushed it for more speed.

"What the hell was that?" Swoop asked.

"Ultimate pain and sorrow." said a voice in the back of the bridge.

The crew turned and looked at Jillian who had tears running down her hard yet lovely face. My god she was so beautiful even now in the grip of grief. Like Jillian, the crew felt that Brig and Korin were lost. Oru was already dying so they did not give him as much thought, believing his lot was cast.

(IN THE PALACE)

When the planet shook, all four of the Guardians in the city knew it was caused by another Guardians G-jen. They can feel the power of a brother Guardian; it is a perk of being on the team so to speak.

Only Jar was happy, because he believed that meant Brig was dead. Rok and Bello looked ill and Jamis had an odd mix of grief and relief. Elon look afraid.

"What was that?" Elon asked.

"It was a Guardian letting go prince Elon. If that blast was aimed at the planet and not away, Grot would be no more." Jamis explained.

"I am going out there; enough of this hanging around waiting bullsh.." Rok growled as Bello cut him off

"I am going with you as well Rok." Bello said in his usual calm way.

"Right, let's saddle up." Rok answered.

Elon gave them a patrol ship so they could get out there fast and away fast if it turned out that there was an enemy waiting for them. Two Guardians were not the foe Elon would want to face, especially these two. They would give even Brig and Korin a run for the money he believed.

Rok piloted the craft because it was set up for a Grot and they are huge. Rok was more the right size for the job so he drove out into the wilds to investigate the explosion that rocked the world.

(IN THE DEAD FOREST)

The fire was gone and Brig was on his knees. Brig was totally blind. The blast stunned Korin, but she was able to revive quickly and tend to Oru. Korin did not know how bad off Brig really was. Brig's eyes were not the only damage; he had the flesh burned off his hands, and one of his ankles was fractured from the pressure of the blast. Worse than any of than; was the fact that Brig gave too much of himself. What that means is; he sacrificed his body to make up the difference in what the energy burst cost. It brought him to near death yet again. If the moment was not so dire Brig might have laughed, he spent a great deal of time sparring with the reaper, luckily he seemed to be winning so far, but how much longer would that last.

"Oru are you still alive?" Korin asked in a shaky tone.

The Wira did not move and answer. Korin put her hand on Oru and she felt and listened for a heartbeat or sign of life but there was none and Oru was nearly the tiny monkey-like creature that Brig first bonded with. Strange only in death did the grip of his transformation let go of Oru. The fact that he was reverting back made Korin believe Oru was dead. Brig closed his blind eyes so Korin would not know and crawled because he was too weak to do anything else based on his condition.

"Brig you look terrible, are you okay?" Korin said at the sight of him.

"Fine." Brig lied.

Korin was not fooled because she could see how messed up her man was. Brig crawled up and put his ear on Oru's tiny chest and listened. Brig did not hear anything, nothing at all. Oru was becoming colder as well.

"You are not going to die on my watch Oru, you are needed by the Kylr as a symbol of change and unity." Brig said.

The human Guardian reached down and hit the hidden clasp on his G-jen and it came away from his arm. Korin flipped out and jumped on Brig.

"NO!!!" Korin screamed as she burst into a typhoon of tears.

Korin hit Brig in the chest and recoil when he opened his blind eye and blood seeped from them. Brig felt Oru's tiny arm and he snapped the G-jen around it. At first nothing happened; but then Oru screamed and wreathed on the ground in agony. Brig held the tiny Wira until he stopped struggling. Oru opened his eyes, alive once more; but at what cost?

"Breeg save Oru again...NO, NO, NO! Breeg no die for Oru. NO!" Oru snarled in genuine anger.

The Wira knew the rules about Guardians and their mighty G-jen. If the gauntlet was removed from a Guardian they died. Oru ripped at the G-jen, but he could not remove it. Korin went to help. Brig grabbed her arm hard and held on to it.

"Not yet Korin, Oru is not fully restored." Brig said.

Korin looked at Brig in confusion, how could he know that? His senses were human again and he was blind and dying, yet he did not look like he was concerned.

"Okay now you can help me retrieve my toy." Brig said.

Oru came and sat down and laid his left arm, the one with the G-jen on it in Brig's open hands. Brig touched the G-jen and Korin stopped him for a moment.

"Wait won't Oru die if you remove the gauntlet from his arm?" Korin asked?

Brig snickered but Korin and Oru did not.

"What you don't trust me?" Brig said as he coughed blood up and it ran down his burnt chest.

Korin took her hands off of Brig's arm and put them on his shoulders instead.

Brig popped the hidden catch that Korin still could not see or even feel. The G-jen came away from Oru and the Wira nearly fainted, and then Oru recovered and smiled. Brigand Sawyer locked the G-jen back on his arm and his right eye was glowing from within.

"Water, Korin bring me some water baby." Brig whispered with a smile on his bloodied and burnt face.

Korin might have died from fright as she watched Brig save Oru. It pained Korin to think that she still had Brig to love when Jillian lost her life in the explosion. Korin would wait until Brig was healthier before she told her man, that his first love had died. Brig was already going to bring hell and damnation down on the heads of all involved with the fail attempt to kill him and Korin and their little party of friends. Korin got up and looked around; there was no water because the bombers pulled the scorched earth scenario. Korin was about to cry when Oru jumped on her shoulder and pointed. High above them was a Grot Scout ship and it was coming lower.

"Quick help me up, now, do it!" Brig yelled.

Oru became a huge gorilla beast again and lifted Brig onto his feet, Korin stood beside them looking upset.

"We must flee, I am too tired and injured to stand and fight and so are you two." Brig said.

"But I feel the energies of Guardians up there in that ship, why do we have to fight them?" Korin asked.

"Korin, we don't know who those Guardians are, and who brought the hell fire onto our heads. You said yourself that the Guardians thought I lost my soul, perhaps they decided not to take a chance and go ahead and kill us all to make sure?" Brig advised her.

Korin looked shocked; she saw Brig's unassailable logic and gave in.

"No more speeky, what Breeg want to do?' Oru asked.

"Can you become a great beast that can run very fast, or are you still to weak?" Brig asked as he nearly swooned.

In response to the question; Oru transformed into a great golden eyed cat, with super long fur. Korin did not waste time she grabbed Brig and jumped on Oru's mighty back.

"Breeg and Korin lay flat; Oru's fur will hide you as I run. Where does Breeg want to go?" Oru asked.

"Take us to the Tarocs Oru." Brig said and then closed his blind eyes.

Above the inferno; Rok and Bello hovered and watched for any sign of life. They were both startled when a hung cat burst from the flames and made for the plains. Rok made a face and then disregarded the cat all together. Bello had a strange feeling about the cat and marked the route it was taking just in case. It would later turn out to be the right thing to do and the only clue to what happened here in the once forest.

Oru put on such a burst of speed; and it nearly took Korin's breath away, and she had to hold the slumbering Brig in place with her arms and leg. If Korin thought Oru's other creature transformations were fast, she was wrong. Oru must have thought the trip was taking to long so he jumped into the air and transformed into a dragon and flew on to the Tarocs herd.

(AT THE PORT)

The Sawyer's Revenge jumped out of light speed and Swoop did not even touch the brakes; he brought the ship in hot, because he was still pissed off, and so was everyone else on board. They all thought Brig, Korin and Oru were dead, so the ship that carried them both body and soul was REVENGE.

Jamis felt the disturbance in the atmosphere and did not know if it was an attack or a friendly craft until it set down like a blur, soft as a babies kiss. Jamis relaxed; there was only one man who could fly like that, Swoop. Jamis was surprised when the hatch opened; that Matho was armed to the teeth, side by side with Tigra; who was also well heeled; came out of the Revenge. They were followed by teams of armed Kylr soldiers that were lead by Milo himself. Jillian had her Glave in hand and the blade was on fire.

"Oh my God, no!" Jamis said under his breath.

Behind Jillian were two prisoners. One was a Karna like the girl up front; the other was a three eyed Chrisalian pirate. What were they doing here, and how did Milo catch them? Jamis walked forward to meet Milo but a blast at his feet stopped him dead in his tracks. Matho looked to be in a murderous rage; therefore Jamis held his place.

"Hold your ground old man, I have no wish to harm you but I am not in a trusting way at present." Matho said.

"I can see that plainly lad. What had happened?" Jamis asked.

Milo and company did not answer; they walked right by Jamis without looking at the speaker a second time. Jillian stopped and looked into Jamis's eyes. Jamis knew without a doubt this day Jillian was going to kill someone...painfully. Jillian looked away and followed Milo up to the palace. The Grot came out of the palace with guns drawn.

"Stop, holster your arms Grot warriors; let them pass and guard them as we go forth." Elon shouted.

Milo knew the prince to be honorable beyond question, and as such he did not suspect him of foul play. Milo approached the prince and spoke.

"A word in private, Prince Elon, if I may?" Milo said.

Elon raised his hand and pointed to the side of the courtyard near the wall. At that place, there were no doors or windows, or way of listening to them. When they arrived in the spot Elon wanted to be in, the prince turned his massive back to the crowd. In this way Elon kept both himself and Milo from having his lips read as they talked.

"We were bombed Elon, from the pirate ship. Brig, Korin and Oru were lost to the fire. The pirates were hired to kill us, or really just Brig I think." Milo said.

"You trust me I take it?" Elon asked.

"Yes, if you wanted us dead, you have done the deed yourself and to our faces. I suspect that the guilty parties are more than one, but I would explore this theory before I name the guilty out of respect for you and us both." Milo said as he looked directly in the giant Grot's eyes.

Elon was shocked at the implications of what Milo had just said. The prince was in no way a fool; he knew this day would come sooner than later. Still Elon did not want to face treason and the punishment that would come from it.

"I understand and I am with you until the end, no matter what the outcome is. You have my word." Elon said extending his giant three fingered hand.

Milo shook the prince's hand and they walked back to the soldiers and continued to the palace. When they arrived, Elon ushered everyone into the huge meeting hall. The hall was currently put away, meaning the chairs and tables were placed neatly off to the sides of the room. Elon directed the Kylr soldiers to place the pirates in the middle of the floor and keep them surrounded. The Grot Warriors filled in the gaps between the Kylr.

There came laughter and loud voices down the hallway that led to the huge hall. Since the doors to the hall were open the king walked right in, the king loved parties and thought one was being planned. The king stopped in his tracks and was going to back out only Jillian was suddenly behind him and so was Tigra. Both of the serious faced women had weapons in their tiny hands. The king and Jar beside him walked into the room and smiled. No body was fooled by the false sense of ease they were trying to project.

"Do you know these scum father?" Elon asked.

"Yes, they are pirates." Elor answered honestly.

   The king thought his moment to discredit his powerful son had come, so he played along. Jar looked ill, though the king did not know why; he was immune to all but another Guardian and then only the very strongest could oppose him even a little.

"Did you hire this trash to kill Brigand Sawyer Jar?" Milo asked in a flat very dangerous tone.

"How dare you question me; I should kill you where you stand!" Jar raged.

"Answer the question Jar." Jillian said as she slipped the Glave between Jar's legs. "Or I can change your religion if you would rather?"

   Jar was a seasoned fighter and an elite Guardian; however if he moved he would be in many pieces instantly. Jar had witnessed Jillian's prowess with the Glave and was not willing to gamble; so he defused.

"Why would I want Brigand dead or anyone else for that matter?" Jar asked.

"Well, for starters; you hate Korin's guts and she took your place as commander. Second, Brig would not allow you to bed Jillian, and you lust after her shamelessly. Shall I continue?" Milo said.

"Watch your mouth boy; consider who it is you're speaking too." Jar snarled.

   Elon walked passed Jar, directly up to his father; where he glared down into his smaller father's face. Elor still feeling cocky shoved off, but Elon did not move at all. The king suddenly felt nervous.

"Father, did you hired pirates to kill guests to our world?" Elon asked.

"No, I did not." The king said truthfully.

"Then I would bet my nuts, that you know who did." Elon raised his voice.

   The king did not rise to the bait. He looked at Elon and put his own plan into action.

"If anyone was killed by the pirates; the blame can be laid squarely on your shoulders. It was you who buried an alien on Grot soil, if you had not insisted on that, none of this would have ever happened. You are the one to take the blame for all that has happened, you endanger the Grot people by your mindless actions." The king accused.

   All the Grot in the room gasped at the kings words. Elon looked at his father and then did the last thing he would have expected. The prince roared with laughter and he continued for some minutes with the mirthful outburst.

"Please, you cannot believe in your tiny pee brain that this would ever work father. You are embarrassing yourself and the entire Grot people acting like an off-worlder. We are the Grot, we are the finest warriors in the universe, and fear is unknown to us. To try to engineer a false burden to place on my shoulders; so that you can continue being king is a disgrace. I have been wrong and I admit it; I have let your lazy useless ass sit on my throne long enough. I challenge you to a duel Elor or you can just step aside. Choose." Elon growled.

CHAPTER 17: WHO'S YER DADDY

Tarc was surprised when a huge dragon landed right in front of him; even more incredible, was the two people hidden in the folds behind the dragon's great wings.

"Tiny? Is he well, he looks like he should have passed on? Were you attacked by the Grot or another hunter?" Tarc asked concerned and more than a little bit angry.

Oru transformed into a great four armed ape and carried Brig into the middle of the Tarocs herd and set him down. Korin wobbled in behind them; she was also in poor shape and exhausted. The grass was trampled down and where Brig was laying on the ground the grass was flat and smooth from a Tarocs bedding down there. The Tarocs were a very clean creature, they did not poop where they slept, so that was not a worry. Korin held Brig gently in her arms and both the bipedal mammals were fast asleep with Tarc and his herd looking after them. Tarc looked at his Tiny and came to a decision he had been dwelling on for a long time.

"Listen to me Tarocs; we have been the prey of the Grot and the Grim'oc for far too long. From here on out we fight for the right to live, we don't run anymore. They have tried to kill our friend and protector; I will not allow any further treatment of this sort to be endured!" Tarc shouted.

The Tarocs were a peaceful race for the most part; however, they were heart sick of being hunted down and killed. They yelled their herd approval of Tarc's words.

Through all the stomping and yelling Oru and the people slept on without any notice of the din going on around them. Korin was lost in a dream of the good times her and her human lovers would have again together. Oru had strange dreams of things he could not know; and of places he had never been. This made Oru unsettled but also enchanted. Brig's dreams were of death; he saw Jillian being burned to death and his friends dying in the hell storm of fire. All Brig wanted was revenge.

The Tarocs moved away from Brig who began to pulsate with crimson energy. Korin's G-jen reacted to protect her; and the slight Kylr beauty was surrounded by a fine green mist. Oru just slept through it unharmed...he was exhausted and sleep was badly needed.

"My God, Tiny is a Guardian, look there is a G-jen on his arm. That means he is the hero that was lost; he is Brigand Sawyer." Tora said all excited.

"Yes child, he is the one. I have known for a while that Tiny and Brigand were one and the same. It was his actions that set him apart; he is about giving, honor and duty." Tarc explained.

Brig opened his eyes two days later and he was dying of starvation. He still could not see; however his Guardian senses were sharper than ever. One more thing; Brig had been moved. Brig knew this because there was water lapping on some rocks now, and when he went to sleep there was only grass in the Great Plains area. Someone was stirring next to him; suddenly a tiny hand was being ran across his face. It felt so good Brig could have cried. There were only two people in the universe that felt like that when they touched him, one was dead and the other was...

"Korin?"

"Yes Brig, I am here darling; and I am never letting you out of my sight again. You are just too much trouble when I am not around to calm you down." Korin giggled as she nuzzled his neck with her face.

Brig rolled onto his back opened his eyes and kissed Korin on the lips so tenderly and passionate, that it took Korin's breath away and made her heart race. They both laid there for a while holding the other tightly. A great deal of the burn damage was totally gone. Brig's hands were close to totally healed, but his eyes were not healed at all. Another voice made Brig turn his head.

"Why Oru no deed, why Breeg no deed when he taky off G-jen?" Oru asked.

"Yes, how did you do that? You should have dropped dead in horrible pain when the G-jen was removed, yet Oru and you have both worn the gauntlet and both of you have removed it; and you're both alive?" Korin inquired confused.

Brig smiled and then laughed deeply. He calmed himself and decided to explain.

"I can't be killed that way Korin, I was already dead. Oru is bonded to me at more than a physical level so he and I can both wear the G-jen as if we were one person. I know this as well; as long as I am alive Oru cannot die either. The G-jen altered his DNA to add some of mine and when I replaced the G-jen on my arm I got some of his, so we are twins after a fashion now. Moreover, my G-jen and yours are removable Korin. Haven't you noticed how much more powerful we are compared to all the other Guardians?" Brig said.

"I actually thought it was all attitude that made us meaner and tougher than them." Korin admitted.

"We are those things and could beat them even if our G-jen was the same as theirs was; but it is not that same. None of their G-jen has a hidden release that can only be removed by the wielder and no other. Look there is yours." Brig said as he ran his hand over her G-jen.

Korin felt were he touched and sure enough it was there. Brig pushed it hard and it did not come off.

"Safety feature I would guess baby." Brig said.

Korin nodded her head forgetting Brig was blind. He smiled because he could sense her agreement with him.

"Remove it Korin." Brig said.

A blind terror came over Korin, she remember what happened when she force the G-jen off of a crazy Guardian, he died a horrible painful death as his cells corrupted and fell apart. Korin started to shiver even though it was as hot as Hades out presently.

"Brig...I am scared; what if you are wrong and I die?" Korin asked.

"Trust, Korin, faith that it will okay. If you can face this fear and overcome it, nothing will ever scare you again ever." Brig explained.

Korin the blue skinned siren of Kyl ran her fingers over her G-jen and found the spot where the hidden release was. She felt it for a few minutes; she shook with fear. Finally, she took a deep breath and opened the G-jen. It came off easily and Korin was dizzy for a second only. Korin looked at her only treasure in her hands and she knew that truth in that moment. Her grandfather Jamis had given her one of the three legendary G-jen and Brig wore the other. Korin began to laugh loudly; Korin was one of three people who could not be killed like other Guardians; that tidbit of knowledge made her very happy.

"One more thing Korin, it cannot be taken away from you either; you are no more vulnerable without it than you are with it. Your powers and abilities as a Guardian do not leave you when the G-jen is removed; they remain intact." Brig said.

Korin smiled and tested the theory. She blasted a piece of driftwood floating on the water, with her right hand. She always used her left hand because the G-jen was there. Now however, there was no arm with a G-jen on it; yet the wood exploded into splinters. Korin giggled again and then stopped and became serious.

"We need to go to the city and make war against our enemies but…" Korin stop in mid-sentence.

Brig smiled.

"But you think I am blind." Brig finished her sentence.

"Brig, you are blind baby." Korin said.

Brig closed his eyes and held up one finger and smiled.

"Watch and be aware." Brig said.

Lightning jumped off Brig's finger and it hit not one splinter but every single one of them and he never missed. A bird flew over head and Brig stunned it gently; he leaped to his feet and caught it before it hit the ground. Korin and Oru were slacked jawed at the display of skill.

"If you under-estimate a foe, then you are dead. When we make war, I am going to act weak to pull in my opponents, and then I am going to crush them for Jillian." Brig said.

"Then I say we get to it lover; there is no way this is going to end well; but they started this shit and I am going to put it to bed...for good." Korin said.

Oru fished for the trio and the Tarocs milled around and grazed on the shore. After a good meal of non-intelligent fish, Brig and Korin looked to be the picture of health after a good meal. Brig told Tarc that he would have the Tarocs moved to another Planet so the grot would stop killing them, Tarc was not sure he wanted to go, despite the Grot; the Tarocs loved this planet and the vast plains. Brig told him to think about it.

"Breeg, Korin let's go pound the bad ones." Oru said.

The trio flew off toward the city with an iron resolve in their hearts and a smile on their happy faces. No matter the outcome or the foe, at least they would meet the challenge together.

(IN THE PALACE)

All the Grot Warriors held their breath waiting to see what the king was going to do. If he chose to step aside; the Grot people would never respect him again. He would be branded a coward. Elon would never let Elor stay on the planet if he refused to fight; if nothing else for his own good. It would be worse if he accepted; Elon would be forced to kill his own father.

"Is there no other option open to me, can I not appeal to the people for another option?" Elor asked.

Elon turned away from his father and looked at the three dozen warriors in the hall, many who were themselves part of the royal family; or from other high ranking families that put them is direct service to the king and prince.

"HA, you fool!" Elor said.

The king pulled a knife and stabbed the prince in the back. Elon did not even flinch. He looked over his shoulder and back-handed the king into the wall nearly half the length of the room; which was vast. The king slammed into the wall and the stone was pulverized. Elon walked over to Rok; who just came in with Bello to report what they saw out there in the burst out area where the forest had been.

"My brother from another mother, do you think you can pull the blade from my back; I seem to be unable to reach it?" Elon asked.

"It would be my pleasure brother." Rok said.

Elon turned around and Rok pulled the knife out and grabbed Elon and held him still. Elon could feel the sudden warm sensation and knew Rok was using his G-jen to partially heal the stab wound. Rok padded Elon on the shoulder. Elon smiled and then walked across the room to where Elor stood looking stunned. Elon had his father's dagger in his hand.

"Are you going to kill me unarmed like a coward?" Elor shouted so everyone heard him.

Elon lunged forward and grabbed his father's wrist. He held his hand still; Elon placed the dagger back in the trapped hand and then stepped back out of range.

"I would not sink to your level; I have never put a blade in to my opponent's back, all my foes went down looking me in the eyes.

Attack me now father, I will not be armed; I will face you with only my open hands." Elon explained.

The king felt he once again had the upper hand. Elor jumped forward and slashed Elon across the chest. Elon hit the king flat in the face with a palm strike; the king was once again slammed into the wall behind him. The king saw the blood running down Elon's chest and was encouraged to attack with fervor. Elon stood in the same spot unmoving; he waited until the king brought his arm up to slash again; and then he moved sideways and brought a left handed chop down on the king's right shoulder, shattering the bones.

"Aaah!" Elor yelled in pain.

The king despite the pain turned into Elon and tried to stab him. Elon stood stock still again until the last moment; and then he punched the king in the jaw with his left hand and then punched the king in the ribs with his right hand. Blood sprayed out the king's mouth. Elon's mighty body shot; must have busted the king's insides up. The king stepped back but this time Elon came with him; Elon chopped down on the king's wrist and the dagger went banging on to the floor. Elon slammed his hands over the King's ears; stunning the king. Elon pinned the king's arms to his body and bear hugged him. The sound of bones imploding and splintering filled the room. When Elon finally let go the king dropped to the floor dead and laid there for all to see. Since the prince used no weapon, no person could dispute his victory, or taint it. Elon was now king.

"Now, Jar it is your turn matey to explain your involvement with these pirates?" Milo said.

"I do not have to explain myself to you lackey!" Jar snarled

A throat cleared behind Jar. All eyes went to the small

speaker standing there smiling.

"I would like to hear your answer Jar, and you do answer to me; so consider that an order." Jamis said pleasantly.

Jar looked very unpleased by the presence of Jamis. Jar still did not have any intention of ratting himself out and facing off with these lunatics.

"I think it is obvious to anyone with a brain that Elor hired this trash to do his dirty work. I care not; because it is none of my business. Execute them and then the matter will be done with." Jar said causally.

"We said we would keep quiet for the money and our lives but if you think we are going to our reward while you live a charmed life; then you have...." Slag started to say.

Jar blasted the Chrisalian pirate to a very good likeness of barbequed beef. The Karna rolled away having better reflexes than his partner; but he was injured as well. Jar took aim at him a second time and his blast was blocked by the orange and pale blue coronas of Rok and Bello.

"My my Jar, killing the witnesses is bad form old bean. Why would you do that?" Bello asked.

Jar did not answer that question; he had already witnessed the king's death and did not want to follow suit; so he blasted a hole in the wall and dove through it and Bello went through the wall after him. Bello returned a few minutes later without Jar.

"He disappeared into the city." Bello said in a dry tone.

Rok was on his knees beside the Pirate trying to heal the burns; they were pretty bad and the pirates life seemed to be leaving him, the Karna spoke Tigra's name. Tigra knelt down by her countryman and listened.

"I have been a blight on my family's honor; so I would have it restored before I die. Jar the Guardian hire us to kill Brigand Sawyer and Korin. Anyone else was just bad luck for them. I also wish my personal fortune to be used to restore the wrong I have done here this day. The remainder of that fortune is to be given to my clan; can you do this for me Tigra the hunter?" Kor asked.

"I will see to it cousin; go in peace to hunt the unknown lands." Tigra said.

Kor gave Tigra a small chain around his neck and explained it would lead her to his treasures. Kor died soon after that with a clear heart and restored honor.

"Kor is to be buried in space; it would be his wish." Tigra said.

"I will see it done." Elon said.

Rok closed up the new kings wounds as the assembled group planned on how to catch Jar. The port and all ways off the planet were block and shut down for the first step; the first of many.

(OUTSIDE THE GROT CAPITOL CITY)

Oru walked into the shadows of the city silently with Brig and Korin on his back. Korin was using private technique she alone knew. It rendered the trio undetectable by surveillance devices and personal as well at night. During the day you could see them; at night they appeared as a dark spot or shadow. The three walked into a shadow beside a warehouse, Brig grabbed a handful on fur and pulled. Oru understood the silent caution and stopped. Brig slide off Oru's back and faded into the shadows. A minute later there was a brief gasp and then a thud. Brig returned and Korin pulled him back up to sit on Oru's back.

"What happened she whispered?" Brig did not answer.

Oru rounded a corner and there laying on the ground asleep and unarmed were the Grot guards for this sector; all three of them. Korin just looked at Brig with a curious respect. Her man was blind as a bat and still weak from the over use of his power; yet, he still was a juggernaut to be stopped; and at this moment, Brigand Sawyer was mad and hurt and heartsick. He was not going to let anything stop his revenge.

"Oru theenks we are being flowed." The giant Wira said.

"Yes, we are not alone. I feel them on our left side flank; they do not know who they are following. They are simply following; they are looking for someone other than us; it is curiosity that makes them follow us; that and they have no sign of their true prey." Brig whispered.

Oru jumped straight up and landed on the top of a warehouse in the shadows. Together the trio watched a solitary person walk under then with a rifle in his hands.

"Matho?" Korin asked.

"Yes, that was Matho." Brig whispered.

They let the young Pirz assassin walk away before they continued on. They all silently wondered what was going on. None of them spoke of it though. When the trio made their way up to the dark side of the palace they found at least two dozen

Grot warrior walking around on guard.

Korin slipped down off Oru's back.

"This time I got it boys." Korin said as she melted in with the
dark.

The Grot watched a soft blue form walk out of the dark; it was
a trim Kylr female and she was more naked then clothed, she
was gorgeous. She held up one hand; there was a flash of green
and all of the Grot were on the ground stunned into utter
unconsciousness. Brig and Oru came out of the dark. Brig was on
the ground walking beside Oru with his eyes were closed and a
smile on his lips.

"Nicely done Korin, they were knocked out while ogling your
body." Brig said.

Oru shifted back into the four armed ape; Brig and Korin
followed the Wira up the side of the palace like a trio of mountain
climbers. They slipped into the palace and went room by room
looking for someone; but none of them knew who that someone
was. Korin knew that she wanted to be by Brig's side and Oru felt
that way as well. When Brig chose an enemy, then they were
with him all the way; until it was finished or they were dead.
Finally, Brig stopped his blind eyes twitched; but did not open. He
pointed at a door. All three of them went to the door and listened.

"Can you believe that Jar had Brig killed?" A husky voice said.

"It is far more likely it was Korin that was the target, Jar lost all
of his power when Brig came to Kyl and even more when Korin
began to share his bed. Jar wanted Jillian to himself; so I would
not put it passed him to kill off the competition. However, Jillian
needs no protector these days what a warrior goddess she has
become." A second voice said.

"Yes, I would hate to be Jar when Jillian catches up to him for killing her lovers; to say he is totally screwed is a gross understatement." The husky voice said.

Brig opened the door and jumped forward and covered their mouths so they could not speak. Rok was shocked and wrapped his huge arms around his tiny hero. Bello pulled Brig's hand away from his mouth and got up and went to door where Korin stood naked in tore up clothing. He stopped and then he picked her up in his arms and held her so tightly. She hugged him back.

"I am so glad you survived little sister, my heart is alight with joy." Bello said.

"Boys, no one can know we are alive; at least not yet." Brig said.

The Guardians looked at Brig; who was still pretty torn up. Rok the more bold of the pair spoke.

"Why not; Jillian will be jacked that you're alive?" Rok asked.

"Yes and you gave us a great gift, you told us Jillian lived, but if you let on we are alive then Jillian may loose her edge and Jar might kill her; therefore, she must not be told, I will make it right when the time comes or not at all." Brig said.

The Guardians did not agree; but Brig even weakened was more than a match for just about anyone. If you added Jillian to that equation; Brig was invincible. The five friends went thru the palace and on the way they took some hooded robes, that were the size Grot children wore. Brig and Korin put them one and walked between the Guardians as they looked for Jillian.

(ELSEWHERE IN THE CITY)

Tigra saw Jar and sent a handful of poison tipped throwing blades at him from the side. The Blades hit Jar's aura and sparked into non-existence. Jar looked and saw Tigra and went to blast her when Matho shot him in the shoulder. Jar was surprised because the bullet went through his shield and hit him squarely in the right shoulder. Matho let a few more go; but Jar increased his aura and the bullets just bounced off the stronger shield of energy. Jar was in trouble; oh, he could handle these two; but that was not the danger. He was found; that would bring others and Guardians as well; that was the main concern.

Jillian was on the roof of the build Jar was backing up toward. She was bidding her time to get a solid shot at killing the traitor; who was responsible for her lover's deaths. Jar was unaware of Jillian, because she was all hunter and predator now. Gone was the prissy little girl she once was. Jillian had changed and with the Glave in her hand, she was as dangerous as any predator in the universe; once more Jillian had no mercy when she came after you. Jillian never like Jar, his lust for her reminded her of the bastard that killed her model friend back on Earth. Never would she let a pig like him touch her body. In fact, Jillian intended to kill him in the next moment or so.

From across the city Oru heard the rifle shots and pointed in there direction. Brig did as well. The group waited the moment it took Oru to become a dragon and then climbed on his back. Oru took to the air and flew like a jet fighter to the area where Jar was being attacked. The former head of the Guardians was ripping the city down to try to get Tigra and Matho. The Merc and the lawman were working together as if they had been doing it for a life time. Jar was having trouble pining them down, they were fast and deadly.

"Down there Oru." Rok said.

Oru circled and dropped like a stone out of the sky just as Jillian dove off the top of the roof at Jar's back. Jar saw her somehow out of the corner of his eye and turned on her and brought his power to focus on Jillian. The Glave in her hands absorbed the bulk of the energies; but not all of it. Jillian was literally suspended in midair blade pointed down at Jar.

"Oh snap, Jillian is engaged with Jar." Korin said in frustration.

There was a sudden pulse of energy and it tossed Jillian into the side of the building like a Rag doll. Korin and Brig were at her side so fast Jar never got the chance to hit Jillian with the finishing blow. Oh Jar sent the killing shot, but the robed figure held up a hand the blow hit it and nothing happened. Jar jumped back in horror. What in the hell could block a blast from his G-jen so easily?

"Korin will she be okay?" Brig asked.

"Yes, Jillian's injuries are only minor the Glave protected her with some of the power Jar intended to use to kill her; ironic isn't it?" Korin said.

Rok and Bello jumped all over Jar; they sent a mass of energy at Jar. Entire buildings were reduced to twigs in an instant.

"STOP!" Brig called out loud.

Bello and Rok stopped; however they did not want to.

"Back away gentlemen." Brig said.

The small robed figure walk out and right in front of Jar and stopped. The person reach up and pulled back the hood with their head still down. Then they yanked off the robe and let it fall to the ground. As the stranger's head came up; so did Jar's heart rate, for both hearts.

"You failed to kill me Jar." Brig said without opening his eyes.

Jar took the closed eyes and body full of scars to mean; Brig was blind and injured and of-course weak.

"Why should I fear a blind man?" Jar said in foolish arrogance.

Brig laughed at him briefly. The other's who were listening; were confused by Brig's reaction until he spoke.

"What makes you think I am blind; you jack ass?" Brig asked.

Jar was about to answer; when Brigand Sawyer took a deep breath and opened his eyes. Jar never even had a chance to scream in terror. From within Brig's blind eyes and open mouth came so much energy that Jar's G-jen was disintegrated instantly as was the arm where is once rode. The senior Guardian lived about fifteen seconds longer. Brig held him close and said the last words he would ever hear.

"You have been weigh and measured and found to be lacking. I will be bedding Kerra as a play toy from here on out you loser." Brig whispered.

Brig threw Jar's dead body at the feet of Bello and Rok.

"Take care of that; won't you?" Brig said.

AFTERMATH:

Jillian woke up in her own bed on Kyl. She was not alone. In the bed with her was Korin who was nude and had her back to Jillian. Jillian crawled close to her female lover and caressed her back from her neck to her butt and then kissed her neck. Korin was deeply asleep and still had the grey signs of serious wounds are her soft blue skin. Someone behind Jillian groaned. Jillian rolled over fast ready to fight; she stopped and began to cry. Brigand Sawyer was laying there beside her with his upper face bandaged. The Earth girl climbed on top of her one true love and kissed him between the deep gut wrenching sobs. Jillian could not even tell when Brig's and Korin's arms wrapped around her and held her tightly. The trio fell back into a death sleep; holding each other so tightly that it was impossible to tell where one person started and the next ended. Oru slept in the entrance to their cavern home. The Wira was no longer willing to let anyone pass by him, not Jamis, not anyone. The steam caves down below the sleeping area; were used the first day that all of the trio were awake at the same time. Korin lead them down there holding Jillian's hand, and Jillian held Brig's hand. The steam caves had an airborne cure for injuries and it made you sleeping at the same time. Korin had these very soft pads she laid down side by side for Jillian and Brig to lay on. When they laid down Korin laid down with them, only instead of sleep they made love as if this was the last time they would ever get the chance. It was so good and erotic; that when the finally finished the last of the passion drive off, they fell once more into a happy coma clinging to each other in the joy of being together.

(FAR AWAY ABOUT GROT)

A solitary invisible ship still watched Grot and made calculations. It had been watching the planet since before Brigand Sawyer was laid to rest and then came back to life. The single alien of incredible age was not concerned about the military of the Grot or the arrogance of the Kylr; who believed they were the ultimate power in the universe. No, however, the alien was concerned by the spark of power and resolve in the tiny pink man who refused to die and the two females who loved him. Together the trio was a match perhaps for even his race. The Wira was another mystery; why would it protect the man and fight like a wild animal in his defense. The Wira were among the oldest and most powerful races in the universe, yet this one acted not like and elder, but a child. Why would he do that, why would he hide his true power; or for that matter, risk his own life for a flea? There were many questions the Dnufer pondered. They are dangerous, their technology is superior to the Kylr in everyway and they want to make or start wars to observe and learn without engaging in the war themselves and risking their own skin. If the Kylr or the Miltoa knew they were out there, they would hunt them down. The Dnufer are not a nice race, they are cowards and they are extremely cruel. They would wipe out an entire race just to complete some stupid experiment.

The Dnufer are smart but they should have made sure the wise and extremely tough Miltoa were not watching them, because they were; at the very moment that the Dnufer was watching Brig fight, the Miltoa was observing the Dnufer and placed a light tag on the cloaked ship for cataloging; like is done to beasts. That is how the Miltoa think of the Dnufer...beasts.

(BACK ON KYL)

In the med lab; in Kyl-prime the capitol, Kerra was in labor with the baby that resulted from the stolen egg and seed she jacked from Brigand and Jillian Robins. What Kerra had not planned on was; just how willful this stolen child would be. Kerra had had other children and they never had she known pain like what she now endured. Kerra cried unashamed and she finally made up her mind to call Brig and Jillian to her side.

"Doctor...doctor, come here please." Kerra gasped.

The entire medical staff rushed in to Kerra's room. She was the most important person in any of their lives, and she was their mentor and a genius on top of that. They were all hopelessly dedicated to Kerra; they loved her.

"I need you to find and bring Jillian Robins and Brigand Sawyer here now, I need them desperately." Kerra grunted out in pain.

The entire med lab staff was on the com with every agency on Kyl. No one could find Jillian or Brig. Jamis was alerted and he called Oru on the special com they set up when they thought Brig was dead, so Jamis could help Jillian thru the hard times. Oru was not happy about having to wake up his bondling and Brig's mates, but he did it because Kerra was a good person and he liked her. Kerra was kindly toward Oru and everyone else for that matter; nothing at all like that bastard Jar.

"Breeg, wakey up, Kerra is sick and she calls for Jilly and Breeg to come." Oru said.

"What, my mother is ill?" Korin asked.

Jillian looked at Korin. Brig just realized that Jillian did not know Korin's story fully. Brig learned the story on the way to liberate Pirz before his second death.

"Brig did you know Kerra was Korin's mother?" Jillian asked.

"Yes, and Jar was her father." Brig said.

"That makes Jamis my grandfather Jillian. I love Jamis and Kerra, but I hated Jar and he hated me back. It was he who tried to have us all killed." Korin said

In a rush the trio washed and dressed and ran out of the hidden upper entrance where Oru was a dragon; sitting on the ledge waiting for them. The short flight took only twelve minutes by dragon transport. Oru set down in the grass in front of the med lab. All the riders jumped down and then Oru became Brig, only the Oru-Brig had golden eyes instead of red-brown.

"Wow Oru, I did not know you could do that; I mean become me." Brig said as they walked in to the lab.

"I am able to do many things you don't yet know about." Oru said in a good approximation of Brig's voice.

Brig looked at him with his blind eyes and a smile broke across Brig's rugged features. Korin had Jillian by the hand dragging her down the hallway to where she knew Kerra would be. Sure enough, Kerra was there; just as Korin knew she would be.

"Hello mother; are you well?" Korin asked.

"Korin my baby, I thought you were dead!" Kerra cried.

Kerra folded in half in pain at that moment and could say no more. Korin rushed to her side and looked at her. Korin gasped as she placed her hand on Kerra's stomach.

"It looks like we have left my new sibling without a father." Korin said.

"What?" Kerra asked between contractions.

"Jar is dead mother. He tried to kill me and Brig; plus Jillian and many others. Brig put an end to the son of a bitch." Korin explained.

Kerra cried a few tears for Jar her long time lover, but not many. She looked up at Brig and then Jillian. Kerra stilled herself and spoke.

"Jar is not the father of this baby; and I am not the mother either." Kerra said.

"How can that be?" Jillian asked.

Brig reached out and touched Kerra's tummy and felt the baby move and then he smiled.

"We are the mother and father Jillian. Kerra took your eggs while you slept after they saved our lives on Earth. Kerra took from me as well and then she fertilized the eggs and implanted it in herself to grow; she spoke of this during the counsel when we first came. Do you remember?" Brig asked.

"Yes, but that was too long ago to carry a baby; unless Kylr carry babies longer than we do." Jillian said.

"SCREAM!"

"I think our child wants out now." Brig said.

"Yes, she does; and no Jillian we do not carry babies longer. I used drugs on my self to slow the process down for the baby's safety and mine while I studied the pregnancy...the infant is very healthy." Kerra said.

Kerra no longer was able to speak; the pain was way too powerful for her to do anything but cry and grunt. Brig was no doctor but he was a country boy and had seen many babies come into the world; although none of them were his three parent children. Still Brig took over.

"Listen to me Kerra, and only me and my voice Kerra. I want you to push when I say so and not until I say so...okay." Brig said.

"Korin get all of these people out of here now!" Jillian shouted.

Korin looked at the staff and pointed at the door; they did not argue; but they were near by if they were needed. Brig and Korin got Kerra sitting up; and then Jillian took Brig's place while he delivered the baby. The baby's head was crowning, so Brig began to coach Kerra.

"Here we go Kerra, push." Brig said.

"OH GOD!" Kerra yelled.

Despite her out burst, Kerra pushed as she was told with her amazing core muscles and the baby's head popped out. Korin gasped and then giggled and so did Jillian.

"Rest and breathe Kerra; then we will have you give it one more good push and then you're done sweaty, okay are you ready?" Brig asked.

Kerra took and deep breath and then nodded her head.

"PUSH...PUSH...PUSH!" Brig chanted loudly.

(Slap, slap...Whaaaaaaa!)

"Well done Kerra and ladies. Here is the prize." Brig said

excitedly.

Brig stood up and held out the baby to Jillian, and not Kerra. Jillian took the infant baby girl; and to Kerra's surprise Jillian laid down on the bed next to Kerra and put the baby on Kerra's chest. Kerra cried.

"Wow, this is really something different; is she my little sister or god-daughter?" Korin asked.

"Neither and both. She is special like you Korin, one of a kind." Brig said.

"More like three of a kind Briggy my love." Korin said as she reached down and lifted the spud up delicately.

Korin held the tiny baby in her own tiny hands and ogled it. The medical staff came in and took care of Kerra. Kerra was concerned because Brig had bandages over his eyes. Brig seemed to read her mind; because he reached up and took the bandages off. All three women gasped. Brig's eyes were all red with black pupils. There was no longer any hint of white.

(THE BABY GURGLED)

The infant was a soft power blue, almost white but not quite. Her eyes were just like Brig's except for the color, as were her tiny hands. The rest of the baby looked to be a tiny version of Jillian in everyway. However, when she got older her hair would be shiny silver just like Korin's.

"Welcome to our family baby...Toffy." Brig said.

MY BOOK COLLECTION:

VAMPIRE HERO SERIES;
BLOOD BY DAY
SHADOW'S REVENGE
SHADOW GUARD

GUARDIAN SERIES:
ENTER THE GUARDIANS: KYL
LOST ON GROT

THE ASHAN CHRONICALS:
BLACK WINGS

THE ELEMENTAL KIDS SERIES: (kids –young adult)
WORLD OF ICE
WAR FOR ICE

THE DRAGON AND FIRE SERIES (PG)
BREATH OF MAGIK

RYAN THE WILDFIRE/ ALBERT YETI: (young adults)
RYAN OF THE WILDFIRE

ADULT VAMPIRE SERIES: (Adult)
VAMPIRE WARS: BEGINNING

THE LORDS OF ORDER SERIES: (PG)
DESTINY'S KEY

LITTLE MONSTERS (Kids) book one

COWARD SERIES:
TAD'S TALE

AN ASSASSIN'S TALE

ONE DARK NIGHT (VAMPIRES)

W. SHANE WILSON

LIST OF TERMS AND PEOPLE:

Earth: planet, home to human race

Kyl: planet gigantic, home to the Kylr, guardians of the universe

Grot: Planet mid sized, home of the war like Grot

Pirz: planet, 4 moons, home of the Pirz

Brigand Sawyer / Tiny: Human, 5'7 150lbs, light brown hair, red-brown eyes, lover of Jillian and Korin, only non-Kylr Guardian

Jillian Robins: Human, 5'9, 110lbs, red-brown hair, blue eyes, ex model, Lover of Brig and Korin

Korin: Kylr, female, 5'7, 115lbs, silver hair, green snake eyes, only female Guardian, lover of Brig and Jillian

Toffy: baby, Jillian's and Brig's daughter. Kerra secretly carried the baby to term without their knowledge. She has the Kylr blue skin and silver hair and perfect health as a bonus.

Rok: Kylr, guardian 7'5, 400lbs giant, Blue skin, slate blue grey eyes, bald like all Kylr males, part of the terrible trio with Korin, and Brig, unstoppable together.

Bello: Kylr Guardian, 6', 185, Blue skin adopted brother of Brig, elegant and deadly

Jar: commander of all the Guardians, Blue, 200lbs, 6', Kerra's lover

Kerra: Kylr genius medical Dr, counsel member, Jamis daughter, Jar's mate, nympho, hottest of all Kylr females

Milo: Kylr flag ship captain, young, strong and willful

Pepper: Kylr female, lieutenant in the Kyl Navy, Milo's little sister, smart as a whip.

Jamis: Kylr elder, speaker for all the Kyl, first Guardian, Kerra's dad, the man who beat the Grot invaders, and kept the peace afterwards, master of all Kyl martial weapons, ultra powerful.

Rob: Kylr Guardian; young, clever cool headed Twin of Dirk. Jamis's personal guardian

Dirk: Kylr Guardian. Young, Mean, dutiful, Rob's twin, Jamis's personal guardian

Scotty: chief warrant officer, 3rd officer (By choice) miracle worker Kylr engineer / grease monkey for the Sawyer's Revenge.

Swoop: Kylr 2nd officer, best pilot in the universe, a little

off his rocker, great friend, Pepper's best friend

Alfie: Kylr boy, burned nearly to death, healed by Sarn, first Official Snake rider of Kyl.

Sawyers Revenge: Kylr flag ship, Milo is the skipper

Brig's Fist: The captain's shuttle from the Revenge, not a toy, gun-ship

Kylr: blue skinned, genetically perfect people, all pretty and fit, cant have babies often, guardians of the universe, Men are bald, women have white silver hair, they are hedonistic people, very sexy because of baby shortage, and they need Earth to save them.

Grot: big scale armored meat eating warrior race, 7'+, 500lbs+, mean, hungry, honorable, combat is everything to them.

Elor: Grot male 1rst commander of Grot forces, later prince and then king, Jamis friend.

Elor 3: Grandson of Grot king Elor, current king of the Grot, mean

Elon; Grot Prince, best fighter the Grot have ever had 10', 600lbs, elegant statesman, reasonable, Jamis close friend.

Pirz: green-ish skin, all shapes and sizes, war like

Mart: rebel leader of the Pirz common people

Matho: a kids who leaner to fight and kill from the Kyl Guardians

Large Marge: Pirz female 7ft, 300lbs, deputy law giver, Matho's GF, all muscle, fast as a pit viper, pretty, single face scar, not personable.

ORU: Wira Monkey, Lasomorph (shape changer) he is Brig's BFF; they are bonded in the soul to each other, friend of Jillian and Korin, Extremely Powerful, and unconditional loyalty.

Grim'oc: huge bear-lion mix, red-black short fur, 1000lbs, 10ft tall standing up, deadly.

Domn: Huge three legged short truck elephant like creature, their poop is the best fertilizer in the galaxy. They are gentle and nearly unkillable.

Tarocs: huge four horned cattle like herd animal, 2000lbs, usually timid and peaceful; however quite fierce and durable if they decide to fight, intelligent minds.

Tarc: the leader of the Tarocs herd, strong and brave Brig's friend, red hide, Grim'oc scar on left front shoulder.

Tora: smaller female Tarocs, Oru's friend

KARNA: CAT HUMAN MIX, HUNTERS OR TRACKER, MERCS

TIGRA; female Karna hunter-tracker, 5'4 112lbs, beautiful, lonely deadly, she is the best of the best, she has never known defeat

SARN: snakoid 4000lbs, 35ft long, Jillian's friend and Alfie's partner. Able to kill or heal depending on what fluid they use.

SLAG: Chrisalian pirate lord: three eyed, evil, mean, 6ft, 245lbs, black hair, gold ears, his own ears were cut off when he was young for stealing.

Kor: Karna, pirate: works with Slag.

Dnufer: Ancient race of near immortals. Elder race, super powerful. White skin, 7ft, small grey eyes. They look like a tall human. They are dangerous, their tech is superior to the Kyir in everyway and they want to make wars to observe and learn without engaging themselves and risking their own skin.

Miltoa: elder race, very powerful and very wise. They let the Kyir look after the peace and keep to themselves; however they are far more powerful than the Kyir are. They look like giant turtles with yellow gentle eyes that

seem to be smiling. They are 5-7 ft tall and 400-800lbs.

ABOUT THE AUTHOR:

   Shane was born Dec 21ˢᵗ, in Portland Oregon, to his mother Toffy Lee Wilson and Oscar Joel Wilson. He has an older sister Cookie Caroline Sinclair and a younger brother Curtis Casey Wilson.

   Shane lives in Vancouver Washington with his Wife of over twenty years, Arlene; and he son Joston and his daughter Jessica Lee.

   Shane races Quads and has won 13 over all championships. Joston has won two and Jessica has one title to her credit as well.

   Shane has studied Martial art for nearly thirty years and has a 5ᵗʰ degree black belt in KAJUKENBO.

   Shane loves to entertain people with his stories; so his beautiful wife bought him a laptop and told him to put them all to paper. It is Shane's goal to write a 100+ books and publish them all. At his current rate; he will reach his goal in under ten years time.

Shane offers this bit of advice:

"IF YOU THINK YOU CAN; THEN YOU ARE RIGHT. IF YOU THINK YOU CAN'T THEN YOU ARE ALSO RIGHT. THEREFORE, NEVER LET ANYTHING BEAT YOU!"

MY PERSON MANTRA IS:

I CAN'T BE BEAT, BECAUSE I WONT BE BEAT.

I MAY NOT ALWAYS WIN, BUT I NEVER LOOSE.

GOD BLESS YOU AND I LOVE YOU.

BTW: STAY TUNED FOR BOOK THREE OF THE GUARDIANS SAGA

www.ingramcontent.com/pod-product-compliance
Lightning Source LLC
Chambersburg PA
CBHW032001240626

47153CB00003B/1075